Summer Winds

SUMMER WINDS

Cliff Schimmels

VICTOR BOOKS™

A DIVISION OF SCRIPTURE PRESS PUBLICATIONS INC.
USA CANADA ENGLAND

Second printing, 1986

Library of Congress Catalog Card Number:86-60858
ISBN: 0-89693-262-1

VICTOR BOOKS
A division of SP Publications, Inc.
Wheaton, Illinois 60187

Contents

CLIFF SCHIMMELS first studied the rural pastorate from the perspective of a boy growing up. Later he stood behind the pulpit and studied the rural pastorate in a new way. It was here that he developed a deep appreciation for the art of storytelling as a form for communicating the Gospel.

Dr. Schimmels is now Professor of Education at Wheaton College, where he continues to tell his stories and also to write books about children, families, and schools. He and his wife, Mary, have three children.

THE WHEATHEART CHRONICLES

Rivals of Spring
Summer Winds
Rites of Autumn
Winter Hunger

The smells and sounds of rural Oklahoma,
a sunset lingering in the West,
a cow grazing on the distant hill,
freshly plowed dirt, diesel smoke,
the growth and harvest of wheat—
it was all a part of my growing.
It is an inseparable part of me still.

To those people who taught me such things
as honesty, sincerity, loyalty, and the honor of work,
to those who opened their lives and invited me in,
I offer these Chronicles as a token of my gratitude
I love you and cherish our times together
both in the present and in my remembering.

Cliff Schimmels
1985

Let no man despise thy youth.

1 Timothy 4:14

1

Second Monday in June 1982

The bus ride from Fort Worth to Wheatheart, Oklahoma can take forever. And for K.D. Garrett, the trip was even longer, because as much as he hated that bus ride, he feared even worse the thought of getting there.

As he sat by the window and looked, without really seeing, he remembered the events which put him on the bus in the first place. When the letter came, sometime in early March, his impulse was to throw it away after casual reading. For one thing, he didn't have time to think about Wheatheart—he was too busy being a scholar of God. He had books to read, and papers to write, and sermons to prepare, and spontaneous dining hall debates to win.

Besides, the letter looked crude. Oh, it was typed in formal letter style, even down to the secretary's initials at the bottom, but the pica type made it look like a high school typing paper.

The content was not all that persuasive, either. Someone named Robert H. Chandler, Pastor of the First Baptist Church of Wheatheart, was going to Israel for nine weeks in the summer. The church needed an interim pastor to live in town, preach twice on Sundays and be available for funerals, weddings, hospital visits, and counseling. Since funds and facilities were meager, the church was looking for a single seminary student with sufficient maturity. The church would provide housing, a modest salary, and an automobile.

But the clincher came when the letter said that K.D. had been referred to Robert H. Chandler by a mutual friend, Joseph Warren. Although the letter did not explain how Mr. Chandler knew Uncle Joe, K.D. was not really surprised that he did. Nearly everyone knew Uncle Joe, retired missionary, retired pastor, and friend of nearly every Baptist in the state of Oklahoma. When K.D. was growing up in Tulsa, he and Uncle Joe attended the same church. When he had felt the call to the ministry while still a high school student, he became one of Uncle Joe's special projects. The two spent hours together. It was Uncle Joe who taught K.D. how to search the Scriptures, how to take a verse and develop its meaning by looking at other verses which related to it. Uncle Joe taught K. D. to love biblical scholarship.

Although K.D. had grown much further in his own theological study and hadn't seen Uncle Joe for several years, he found the memories stirred by the letter refreshing; and for that reason, he didn't throw it away immediately. Rather, he filed it in his devotion Bible where he sometimes kept little special notes to himself. That way, for the next several days, he kept bumping into the letter on a regular basis, reminding himself that someday soon he would have to respond.

Finally, one Friday afternoon when he could spend time away from studies to think a few weeks into the future without feeling guilty about it, he sought out some counsel.

He first stopped in at Mr. Raley's office. Mr. Raley, who taught Pastoral Ministries, was one of the few professors on the whole seminary campus who did not have a doctorate; but he did have many years of experience as a pastor in several churches. He also had pertinent suggestions for would-be pastors and personal stories to document those suggestions. Besides that, he always had time to talk.

Although K.D. had an A in the class (he had an A in all his classes, for that matter), Pastoral Ministries was not one of his favorites. He enjoyed Mr. Raley and his stories, but he felt the whole thing was a little on the light side for something as serious as seminary education. But he still wanted to get Mr. Raley's impressions of the Wheatheart opportunity.

Mr. Raley was excited for him and, as usual, he had a personal story about his own interim pastorate during his seminary days— how he had gone into a little community out in west Texas feeling so capable and efficient, and how he had come away having learned the lessons of humility and more careful Bible study. The plot itself was simple and a bit trite. K.D. and all would-be ministers had heard it many times before; but some of the little personal accounts sandwiched in for effect had a local-color flair which made the story worth listening to.

Something in Mr. Raley's tone and word choice made the people alive, vibrant, and even noble in their sense of community tradition. K.D. even found himself smiling a couple of times, and he left the office actually happy that he had at least kept the letter in his devotion Bible.

But he wasn't through with his research. He walked across campus to the cluttered office which walled in the girth, if not the energies, of Dr. Casper, hermeneutics professor and published author, whose scholarship was renowned even outside the denomination.

For K.D., Dr. Casper was more than a teacher. He represented the success of study—a model of scholarship. Although he had not always known it, K.D. knew now that this was what he wanted to become. He wanted to stand above the mundane. He wanted to use his mind to investigate, to evaluate, to bring clarity to the issues which were problems to serious scholars of the faith.

He realized that such activity would invite controversy; but as he had observed Dr. Casper for the past two years, he was even enticed by the controversy itself.

By now, K.D. had been in that office so many times he was actually comfortable with the clutter. He navigated his way past the homemade bookcases, the piles of journals and books lying in organized heaps in the middle of the floor, and the art and artifacts stuffed in corners to remind Dr. Casper where he had been. He found the scholar hunched over a miniature table which served as his desk. Although the day was warm even for springtime in Texas, Dr. Casper had turned up his suit coat lapel tightly around his neck as if to show that he was cold or trying to achieve isolation. K.D. slid quietly into the chair behind the desk and waited long minutes until the professor broke his concentration from reading enough to feel someone else's presence in the room.

When he looked up, he recognized K.D., did not change expression, did not loosen the grip on his coat collar, and said only, "Yeah?"

As quickly as he could, K.D. explained the letter and the invitation. Dr. Casper looked back at his book, put his finger on the spot where he had quit reading, and said into his upturned collar, "Don't go. You've got too good a mind for that kind of stuff."

K.D. probably looked a bit quizzical, but since Dr. Casper did not respond to looks, K.D. asked, "What do you mean?"

Dr. Casper flipped through the book as if he were surveying what was ahead and said, "I tried something like that once myself. Got talked into it. Worst mess I ever experienced. People in those little churches in farm towns wouldn't understand a biblical principle if it bit them on the sole." Neither smiled at the pun and Casper went on calmly. "Stay here this summer. I'll get the school to put you on as my assistant. You can spend the summer reading my papers and helping me with a research paper." With that he went back into the book and his upturned collar, and K.D. left as quietly as he had come in.

K.D. still had one more person to consult, the most important one, Rebecca. Despite his respect for the two professors with the two different opinions, K.D. still respected Rebecca's opinion more on those matters where he chose to seek her opinion, and this was one of those matters. K.D. had known Rebecca for less than nine months, since she was only a first-year student at the seminary, from

Forth Worth even; but in that time he had grown to respect her thoughts. Perhaps some people would not have found her as wise as K.D. did, but since he first found her beautiful, he also found her wise in those matters where he sought her wisdom.

That night, the two walked hand in hand along the tree-lined streets bordering the seminary campus, laughing frequently. They laughed at each other, at their friends, and at their professors, but mostly they laughed because they were young and together.

Somewhere in the midst of all the togetherness, K.D. paused in his laughter long enough to tell her about the letter and about Casper's alternative offer. She waited for him to say more; but when he didn't, she asked, "What are you going to do?"

It was his turn to wait. "I don't know. I really don't. I know what I would like to do. I would really like to help Casper with his research. Doesn't that sound exciting, to spend one whole summer studying one profound idea in depth and intensity? Maybe even discovering something new that no one has ever thought of before? Discovering something that would make a real contribution to the kingdom of God?" He paused just to marvel at the possibility.

She nudged him again into the moment at hand. "But what are you going to do?"

"Well, that's what I am going to do," K.D. said. "That's what I'm best at, and it's no sin to spend your time doing what you're best at.

"Besides, this is where I am going with my life anyway. What an opportunity! I would be wrong to do anything else this summer."

After they had walked in silence long enough to close most conversations, Rebecca asked quietly, "K.D., tell me about Uncle Joe."

They sat on a bus stop bench for nearly two hours while he told her about Uncle Joe, and when he was finished, he went home and wrote to Robert H. Chandler saying that he was interested in talking about the summer internship at First Baptist Church of Wheatheart, Oklahoma. He mailed the letter that night before he had time to change his mind.

The correspondence which followed in the weeks to come only

reminded him that he had acted impulsively. After that first exchange, Robert H. Chandler disappeared and all the other letters from Wheatheart were signed simply, "Brother Bob." Some of the letters brought factual data: the size of the congregation, special events scheduled through the summer, the church secretary's work hours, the length of his stay, and the name of his landlady, Mrs. Strommer, widow. Other letters brought subjective kinds of material and were more disturbing. In country clichés and pica type, Brother Bob tried to describe the indescribable—the nuances and the people of a community so strange to K.D. that he couldn't even imagine it. At no time had he ever known such people as those who came through in the letters; and these foreigners interrupting his life as a scholar caused him to resent even the memories of Uncle Joe which had driven him to accept the offer.

To other people, he tried to portray an optimistic image. He told his fellow scholars of the great opportunity to express his own scholarship in a summer full of sermons. He spent extra time in the library, researching points, and reading about some of the great preachers through the ages. He sought special time from all his professors, looking for little hints which might help him better fulfill his duties. He took care of all his business so that he could get away by the second Monday in June. But even then, he would miss Brother Bob by more than a week. He packed two suitcases full of books, and that was only the bare necessities: study Bibles, a Greek lexicon, two volumes by Spurgeon, a joke book written by a Baptist preacher in Ohio, a minister's manual—a single volume which seemed vital.

It was a good front and fooled everybody, except Rebecca. On those evenings they spent together before finals, during the study breaks they thought they could afford, she would almost always move the conversation to Wheatheart. From Brother Bob's letters, they built images of the people and the scenes almost as if they were writing a script; but just to loosen the tension she would create a background of humor and absurdity. They laughed about the possible scandal of his living alone with the Widow Strommer. She wondered who would have to build the fires for the early service and who would clean the spitoons in the foyer. She asked where he would hide in case of a wild Indian attack, and more seriously she wondered how often the mail would come to town—so that he would know that she expected regular letters.

The anticipated summer gave K.D. something to discuss with his parents during the weekly telephone ritual. Although he still looked forward to those calls simply because those people were his parents, he had almost run out of conversation material during the past two years.

For one thing, his parents represented his past, something he once was but could never be again; and he could no longer talk to them about that world.

But he couldn't tell them about his new world, his real world of ideas and research and thought; so they spent their long-distance budget talking about shallow things—housing, health, and the weather.

Now that he was going to Wheatheart for the summer, he could at least supply them with information about such things as housing and weather; and he could respond to his mother's anxieties and advice.

But even that didn't help ease the dread that second Monday in June when he studied his thoughts and the Oklahoma countryside from a Trailways bus window. Even the bus ride was an insult. K. D. Garrett had never ridden a bus before—he had always flown. Twice, he even flew first class, just enough to know that someday he would always fly first class. But when he called the travel agents to ask about flight schedules to Wheatheart, he only amused them. Maybe it was his own fault. He should have kept his car; but he had sold it to pay tuition, thinking he would not need a car again until he graduated. The bus ride was the best he could do, but he was determined not to enjoy it.

The Red River which creates the border between Texas and Oklahoma was indeed red with mud which had blown in from the barren farms across the prairie. The Arbuckle Mountains which line Interstate 35 in the southern part of the state did not look like mountains at all but just bare piles of rock growing out of prairie grass. The little towns in the distance, hooked to the interstate thoroughfare by nothing but a sliver of concrete, looked desolate. In Oklahoma City, the heat from the sprawl was even fiercer than in the countryside. But during the two-hour layover there, K.D. sat outside on a bench in half shade, rather than going inside and mingling with the bus crowd.

As unpleasant as the trip had been so far, it was even worse as they turned north and west along the two-lane roads and through the small towns to Wheatheart. K.D. was actually an Oklahoman, a thought that sometimes gave him a little pride, but he was from Tulsa—urbane, sophisticated, ambitious. Tulsa seemed a million miles away from that endless semi-desert he was crossing.

If he hadn't been so upset, he might have noticed the summer activity—the combines out in the fields just beginning to gather the wheat so rich that some poets have called it gold. But K.D. saw only the heat waves rising out of the asphalt highway, looking like dew falling up. He slid back into his seat and remembered his past and looked forward to his future—not to Wheatheart but to the end of the summer.

Sunday Evening at Seven

The people in Wheatheart had made plans for K.D.'s arrival.

It all began on a January day, when Charlie Brady started to write his monthly contribution to the church and by force of habit wrote 1980 instead of 1981. While he was in the process of correcting the mistake, and muttering some unchristian comments about his mind and old age, he suddenly remembered that Brother Bob came to Wheatheart in 1956. "Wait a minute," he said. "That's twenty-five years ago. Brother Bob has been here for twenty-five years."

For the next few days as Charlie Brady traveled around town, and he was always traveling around town, he frequently mentioned his discovery. Right in the middle of one of his stories from the past, he would stop and mention, "Do you boys realize that Brother Bob has been here twenty-five years?" Of course, his reminder surprised everybody. It even surprised, but did not necessarily deter, those people who had always felt that Brother Bob was just using Wheatheart as a stepping stone while he prepared himself for bigger and better things.

Soon everybody had picked up on Charlie's bit of news, and it became about the hottest piece of conversation in town. All up and down Main Street people would casually mention it as they talked about more important issues such as lack of rain, farm prices, the prospects for next year's football team, and new babies. The preacher's tenure was reported at least five times a day for a week around tables of the Dew Drop Inn Cafe and around the bolt bins of the John Deere store.

Regardless of the place, the response was the same. "Twenty-five years? Why, I declare, it seems like yesterday."

"I guess you're right. He married Abe and Mary Ruth. I do remember that."

"It's hard to imagine. He still looks just like he did when he first came."

"A quarter of a century sure goes fast when you look back on it."

"Sure, I remember it. He came right in the middle of the fifties, during those dusty years when things were pretty hard."

"Yep, and they may get hard again if we don't get some rain, I'm telling you. That wheat out there ain't rooted deep enough, and come March she just may be blowing all the way to Texas."

"Maybe that would be a good deal. Those guys down there would have to cut it and we wouldn't have to buy all those high-priced parts to get our old combines ready for harvest." With that everyone would laugh to ease the tension, and then the conversation would glide into more usual and gentle topics, ones which didn't remind the participants of the harsh realities of fleeting years.

After a few days, somebody had a great idea. Since several people claimed responsibility, no one seemed to know for sure who started it, but it didn't matter. The idea spread rapidly, maybe even more quickly than other ideas because this one was a secret. "Let's buy Brother Bob a gift," most of the town said almost at once. "Let's show our appreciation."

About then somebody else thought of the perfect gift. "Let's send him and his wife to Israel. Wouldn't that be the perfect gift for a preacher with twenty-five years experience?" And they all agreed, partly because they had heard of people in other towns who had been to Israel; they wanted someone from Wheatheart to go too.

So the idea took deep root and grew faster than sunflowers in the turn rows, and soon a community-wide collection was underway. Anybody could participate, and almost everybody did. Of course, all the Baptists made their donations; but the merchants up and down Main Street and the widows Brother Bob visited in the hospital, and the farmers out in the community who didn't come to church except for weddings and funerals, all wanted to show their appreciation as well. Even the Methodist preacher made a contribution.

At first, the whole idea was supposed to be a secret; but how can you keep a secret from a man whose whole life is listening to other people's secrets? And how can you take up a collection for a man who knows the most about taking up collections? So Brother Bob soon found out and he participated in the details of his gift as much as the others. But this was still a project of the people. They thought of everything. They took up the money, bought the tickets, arranged tours, and even bought Brother Bob and his wife, Leah, a new camera and several roles of film.

But in their enthusiasm for details, they left out one small thing. They forgot to think about what they would do for a preacher during the nine weeks Brother Bob would be gone. He smiled when he mentioned it to them and told them that he would take care of it. He didn't tell them exactly how he would take care of it, but that was not unusual for Brother Bob. He frequently went about duties outside of Wheatheart, such as denominational matters, without telling anyone what he was doing or how he did it. He just took care of things efficiently and quietly, as if he didn't want to bother them with details.

No one knew that he had talked with Uncle Joe or had written to K.D. until Brother Bob himself found the appropriate time for the announcement.

For him that time was during the calm of late May, when the passions of spring had ebbed and the urgencies of summer had not yet begun. School had been out for almost two weeks, so no one was thinking about football games or band practice or even classes and homework. The city crew had already patched the potholes in the streets from last winter's weather and traffic. All the gardens had been planted, and some people had already begun to get a few fresh peas and radishes from those plots with lots of sunshine.

Out on the farms, the first cutting of hay was in the barn, the calves had all been born, the spring chickens ordered from the hatchery had already begun to grow combs big enough to distinguish the roosters from the pullets, and the combines had been repaired and were standing in a ready position.

With all this completed, a calm fell over Wheatheart. But it was a restful calm, not like the calm of late August when the activities stop but the hearts of the people pound on anxiously. While the calm in August is empty with reflection and regret, the calm in May is filled with expectation and hope, because everyone knows that as soon as the summer winds turn to the south and the sun is hot, those acres and acres and miles and miles of wheat now gently blowing in the breezes will grow brighter and brighter yellow, and will ripen, until suddenly, harvest erupts.

In the midst of that May calm, to add even more quietness, Sunday came, and at the end of the day, Sunday evening came and brought serenity.

The traffic slowed to almost nothing except for a stray car or two clattering along the highway with people just passing through. A few porch swings creaked as some people used the last minutes of daylight to finish reading the Sunday paper. Doc Heimer's old dog, Spencer, got up from his usual spot in front of the drugstore on the corner of Main Street and the Highway and went home. And the fragrance of lilac blossoms filtered through the air, bringing peace to all the senses.

About the only interruption to the peace came from the two churches that had any kind of Sunday evening services anymore. The Pentecostal Holiness Church down in an old converted store on Main Street directly across from the Dew Drop Inn Cafe had a full service, with lots of music and singing and laughter and praise, and an hour-long sermon.

Further up Main Street, almost all the way to the high school, in the First Baptist Church, Brother Bob stepped to his pulpit at exactly seven o'clock and started the service with prayer. Brother Bob always started the service promptly. It was a part of his nature, something the people expected from him. And he knew it was exactly seven o'clock because he had cut a hole in the top of the pulpit and installed a clock so he could tell the exact time without bothering anyone.

After the opening prayer, Mrs. Garland led the congregation in singing stanzas one, two and four of three hymns. Although she had a nice voice and was animated and lively, Mrs. Garland wasn't the regular song leader. Jeff Devine, the pharmacist down at the drugstore was, but he had gone down to Canton Lake to water ski that afternoon, and hadn't gotten back in time. As the permanent substitute, Mrs. Garland was always ready for situations like this.

Four of the younger kids, fifth- and sixth-graders, took up the offering. On Sunday evenings, Brother Bob always had these boys take the offering. Sometimes they missed a row or dropped a plate, and they were even capable of breaking out in a giggle for no apparent reason; but Brother Bob still thought that their education outweighed the interruptions. Besides, the church enjoyed them as much as they enjoyed themselves.

For special music, Carol Anne Bray, Mrs. Strommer's granddaughter, sang, "Come and Dine." Everyone always expected her to sing well. After all, she was majoring in music down at the college in Alva. But this night, because she sang so well, or the words were the right ones, or the Spirit came, the congregation was moved into quiet stillness, and tears came into the eyes of some of the women, and some of the men said, "Amen."

Brother Bob, hearing the stillness, waited patiently in his chair beneath the baptistry painting and let the silence prick the emotions even deeper. When the quiet ripened into fullness, he stood and moved gracefully to the pulpit. Brother Bob was a graceful man, still youthful and athletic in many ways—his movements, his hairstyle, his smile—but was mature in other ways—his waistline, his reserved demeanor in crowds, and his choice of a black Bible instead of the red one he had used when he first came. But as he paused to glance at his notes and find the right reading, Mrs. Strommer stood to her feet and said in the loud, shrill voice that was her normal tone, "Preacher, Preacher."

Brother Bob looked up and smiled at her.

She went on. "I hate to say it because she *is* my granddaughter, but I think all of us got something out of that last song. I really do. I know I felt it myself. Why, I just feel like worshiping, and I think before we let all this get away from us, we ought to sing a couple of stanzas of 'How Great Thou Art.' "

Brother Bob smiled again and said, "Well, I was thinking that myself, Mrs. Strommer," and stepped back from the pulpit. The congregation stood, probably because Mrs. Strommer was already standing as if it were the thing to do. They sang from memory the four stanzas of "How Great Thou Art," some heartily along with Mrs. Strommer, some more quietly. But all sang as if they meant it, and the words themselves echoed off the ceiling and bounced around the room until they found a place to lodge.

The second time Brother Bob walked to the pulpit, he was in a lighter mood and he smiled at his congregation. "I want to make an announcement," he began. "I want to introduce you to someone who isn't even here—your pastor for the summer." He paused as if the announcement would surprise everybody, and he looked for the expressions of their faces. But they didn't come. The announcement wasn't really that much of a surprise. Earlier in the month, Brother Bob had talked with Mrs. Strommer about K.D.'s living arrangements, and she had spread the news. By now, most of the congregation and even the town, for that matter, knew more about K.D. than the pastor did, because they knew both what he knew and what they imagined.

But he told them anyway. "Our new pastor is a Tulsa native, a graduate of our fine Baptist college, and a student at Fort Worth Seminary." Again he paused to accent the significance of those credentials before he changed his style from official to friendly. "Now, folks, this is the first time this young man has ever pastored.

He will be new. He will be green. He will be scared. But all of us have been new and green and scared sometime in our lives. We get over that because we have Christ as our light, and we have fellow Christians as our companions. Now this young man is going to need lots of love and understanding, but I know you are going to give it to him and y'all are going to have a wonderful summer. It sounds so good I just may stay here myself." Everyone laughed, partly because they knew he didn't mean it and partly because they wanted him to know they had heard him.

As the mood and tempo changed, Brother Bob opened his Bible and read, "Let no man despise thy youth; but be thou an example of the believers in word, in conversation, in charity, in spirit, in faith, in purity."

With that for a text, he made his sermon around the announcement of K.D.'s coming so that the whole service fit together like one giant plan. The outline was strong, I. The Vision of Youth. II. The Energy of Youth. III. The Purity of Youth; and the illustrations were pertinent because they were personal little accounts from Brother Bob's own past when he was himself a young pastor, some which dated back the whole twenty-five years and some which went back only three or four years; but since even those stories were about him during a different era, they were about his youth.

As he brought the message to a climax, he finished by quoting Rudyard Kipling's poem "If"—all of it, word for word from memory, and some of the old-timers moved their lips in synchronization with the words as he spoke.

Throughout the sermon, the congregation all listened to the same words, yet they heard different messages . . . .

Abe Ericson heard only the wisp of a leftover dream; instead of filling his mind, the words emptied it. Recently Abe had lost his only son in a terrible accident. Killed in a football game, his son would never be a youth but only a dream.

Although Abe was not a big man, his shoulders and his arms made him look like a man of the soil, and his hands acted as a badge to his industry. They were big hands, rough and practical, built for working, for pounding and digging, lifting and shoveling; and this evening, they trembled during church.

Mary Ruth, his wife, noticed the trembling, slid closer, and with her own hands, the hands of a farm woman but dainty by comparison to his; stilled her husband's trembling. Mary Ruth had lost a son too; but she could cry when Abe couldn't, and because of that she comforted him.

* * * * *

Mrs. Garland, sitting on the front pew because of her position of responsibility through the service, listened actively. She nodded in agreement, scribbled the main points on the back of a bulletin she had carried in her Bible for more than a month, and smiled at the illustrations. Yet inside, the obvious reality that she was growing old gnawed at her stomach lining. She didn't have to think of that. She could have thought about her own success as the popular high school Sunday School teacher. Or if she had been more objective, she could have thought of her own beauty. Although she was not as breathtaking as she once had been, she was still an attractive woman. She dressed in the latest styles, she took care of herself, and she worked at being beautiful. But in spite of what everyone else said, that wasn't enough. Her husband, Scott Garland, third generation John Deere dealer and one of the best known and most successful men in all of Wheatheart, had trouble staying home. "Away on business," he lied to her, and "Away on business," she lied to the rest of the community when someone would comment that they weren't together much anymore. It was convenient to say but hard to utter, because she knew Wheatheart well enough to realize that everyone knew the truth. Regardless of what she might have wanted to tell herself, the evidence was there. She was growing old, and the vision, the energy, and the purity was gone forever. Throughout the sermon she was lively and lonely.

* * * * *

Vince and Elizabeth Ann Benalli held hands, smiled at each other with their eyes, and acted like newlyweds. But they weren't. Married more than twenty-five years, they had just recently discovered what it meant to be married, because each had discovered what it meant to love God. Now they cherished life and each other. Since Vince enjoyed being the high school principal and didn't want to be anything else, he enjoyed the sermon and drew memory pictures of students past and present into every sentence and every illustration. Since she was the principal's wife and didn't want to be anything else, Beth Ann helped him remember as much as she could, and never once thought of herself as the bank president, recently retired.

* * * * *

Charlie Brady listened to the sermon with half of his attention and guarded his new Stetson hat on the pew beside him with the other half. But Charlie could do that because he was an expert conversationalist. He always listened with one ear while he gathered his thoughts and remembered the story he would tell when he could next jump into the talk. Because of his storytelling, Charlie was a legend, and he knew it. So he was really just helping keep the legend alive.

Since the pastor was talking about youth, Charlie wondered if he knew anybody who qualified. He knew about teenagers—people who wore long hair and took dope and demoralized the country. But youth was a different matter. Those were the people who went to church and did what their parents told them, and Charlie didn't know many of them. Or if he did, he didn't think about them much because they made dull stories.

Besides that, Charlie had an even bigger interest in the announcement. Because he had been around the church almost longer than anyone else, and because he didn't have much else to do, he had volunteered to take K.D. around and help him get acquainted with the community, and maybe even tell him a story or two.

* * * * *

Delbert Goforth listened to the words from the front side of age instead of the back. He saw himself just entering youth, and he heard the sermon not as a reminder but as a promise. Two weeks ago he had graduated from Wheatheart High School. He really hadn't distinguished himself much, but when he walked across the stage to get his diploma and shake hands with Mr. Casteel, the superintendent, and Mr. Garland, the school board president, he got a standing ovation. It started somewhere among the seniors themselves; but because it seemed like such a good idea, the reaction spread and soon everyone was standing and clapping. Delbert's whole head turned red, all except that blotch of ill-kept black hair at the top. He knew why they were applauding, but he didn't know the deeper reason. A couple of weeks before graduation, he had run the 5,000-meter race down at the state track meet. He didn't win the race. In fact, he didn't even finish. But he did lead it for the first 4,000 meters, and because of his pace, his companion, Chuck Murphy, not only won, but set the new national record. But Delbert still didn't know why those people applauded at graduation. They didn't applaud the football players who had won the state championship last fall. But it didn't matter. They could applaud if they wanted to. Sometimes people needed to do things like that just to get it out of their systems.

* * * * *

Carol Anne Bray sat beside her grandmother, listened to Paul's counsel to Timothy, and remembered a promise she had made to the Lord once that she would marry a minister.

Mrs. Strommer took a special interest in the sermon because she had helped the church get ready to hear it. This church needed her for just things like this, and the young minister, despite all his youth, was going to need her too. So instead of marking down what he had to offer her, she marked what she had to offer him—a room in her basement with clean sheets and free laundry service and the kind of wisdom you can only get from someone who had already lived through things. As she listened, she occasionally looked with pride at her granddaughter who had sung so well and wondered if the young man had a steady girlfriend.

* * * * *

That evening service was a good one, and everyone said so the next morning when they met at the post office or at the Dew Drop for a cup of coffee or out in front of the drugstore at the corner of the Highway and Main Street. "Brother Bob was right. That young man, what's his name—K.D. something, will probably be good for us this summer. It doesn't hurt to sweep the floor with a new broom once in a while."

"Yes," Charlie Brady would remind them as he heard them talk. "That may be true. But just remember, the old broom knows where the dirt is." And then he would chuckle at his own humor. He was still chuckling two weeks later when the Trailways bus brought K.D. Garrett to Wheatheart and deserted him at the drugstore at three o'clock in the afternoon.

The New Reverend

K.D. had thought the bus itself a bit too warm for comfort, but when he stepped out into the Oklahoma sunshine, he gasped for breath. Just before the bus had pulled to a stop in front of the drugstore, he had rebuttoned his shirt collar, tightened his tie and put his jacket back on. Now that he was outside, he wished he hadn't. The southern summer winds, which had already blown across hundreds of miles of ripened wheat picking up heat all the way, stung his skin. Immediately great bubbles of perspiration swelled from out of the pores on his forehead and dropped down, staining his coat lapel.

He moved aside; if he stood in that spot too long, he would dissolve into a puddle. The bus driver, still in his complete uniform, stepped out behind K.D., lit a cigarette and started puffing hard so as to get the best out of it before he got back on the bus. As if he didn't even notice the heat, he swung open the huge cargo door in the belly of the bus, pulled out K.D.'s case full of clothes and set it gently on the sidewalk. Then he pulled out each case of books, straining as if he was angry about their weight and dropped them beside the other case.

Having finished his chores, he returned to the door of the bus, stood with his fingers wrapped around the cigarette, puffed hard three or four times, and with the gestures of a circus star, flipped the cigarette into the gutter more than twenty feet in front of him. Then he stepped back into the bus, and soon he and and the bus both were gone, leaving K.D. stranded right in the middle of Wheatheart with not one thread of connection to anything of his past.

K.D. surveyed the consequences of his March impulse. To his left, he looked into the open door of the drugstore. A three-bladed overhead fan rotating slowly at least made a cool noise; but other than that, the place looked hot. K.D. recognized display cartons and promotional posters like he had seen in the stores in Fort Worth, but nothing else looked familiar. The floor, built of narrow boards, had been stained a dark brown through years of too much floor sweep; the foot traffic through the middle of the aisle had worn the dark shiny. The display cases themselves were framed in the same wood but looked newer because they had escaped the floor sweep. The glass in the display seemed clean enough, but through the years had been scratched and banged so that now most of the items inside seemed distorted by the scratches.

Looking north beyond the drugstore, K.D. squinted through the heat, seeing but not really questioning what he saw—the old movie theater with its crumbling marquee propped up with two-by-fours, the Red Bud parking lot with only three cars, the fire station with an old-time fire truck parked half on the sidewalk. As K.D. looked across the street, he was able to make out the two churches. The nearer one was a pleasant red brick building flanked with cedars. The other, a little farther up Main Street, seemed to be an old steep-roofed white wood building with Gothic looking stained-glass windows and a bare yard which apparently served as a parking lot.

Something inside of K.D. told him that one of those would be the First Baptist Church, and he cast his vote for his preference. On past the churches were homes that sat back among scattered, puny elm trees with a few evergreens mixed in for color.

Up the hill at the end of the street stood the high school. K.D.

knew it was the high school mostly because it looked like one but also because of the flagpole out front.

Now he turned and looked to the south. Just across the highway on both sides of the street were banks. Although the buildings weren't the modern architectural experiments like those which house the banks in Tulsa and Fort Worth, they were still stately and brought a sense of dignity that was incompatible with the rest of the town. On both sides of the street, storefronts of glass and steel had been stuck on old buildings, leaving the old up above. In some places, canopies of old buildings still almost covered the sidewalks, but in other places they were deteriorating into half coverage or had disappeared altogether. With his casual survey, K.D. only noticed one sign—Dew Drop Inn Cafe—and he almost smiled at the thought of eating in something called the Dew Drop Inn Cafe. Since he didn't know anything about Wheatheart, he barely noticed the bright green and yellow equipment stacked in the John Deere yard at the south end of Main Street.

He also hardly noticed the trucks lining the Highway, some going east and some going west. Anyone with any experience on the prairie would have seen the trucks first. They were huge trucks which strained with their loads even as they sat parked. Although tarps stretched tight across the tops covered the loads from view, the sideboards of solid wood and steel attested that these were grain trucks, waiting in line to get to one of the elevators at each end of town and dump those precious loads of wheat and go back to the fields for more.

Since nothing in his past would help him see this, K.D. didn't dwell on the trucks, nor did he distinguish the sounds coming from the elevators, sounds of huge machinery at work, and people shouting one-word instructions to each other. He only looked up and down Main Street and found it devoid of life—except for the huge furry dog lying asleep close enough to the doorway of the drugstore to catch what cool breeze might come from the three-bladed fan, and two gnarled men across the street in the shade of the bank canopy, sitting hunched down like baseball catchers with their backs braced against the wall.

One was whittling, and the other was whirling his hat in the air with his hand and talking with huge mouth movements.

As K.D. was watching, the whittler got up with some degree of purpose and ambled down the street toward the Dew Drop Inn. The other put his hat on and wandered across the street toward K.D.

"You the new Rev?" he yelled while he was still in the middle of the highway.

"I beg your pardon?" K.D. was used to southern accents, but this was not the mellow, reserved, elongated tones that K.D. knew. It was shriller and more nasal, and he had to ponder a moment to know for sure what he had heard.

"You the new Baptist preacher?" The man asked again with the same sound.

By hidden instincts, K.D. snapped to attention spiritually and physically. "I am Pastor K.D. Garrett, the interim here," and he held out his hand to the stranger.

The gnarled man with the big hat and the huge mouth movements walked on past, not so much as if he were rude, but rather as if he were busy. "I'm Charlie, Charlie Brady. I'm supposed to pick you up and nurse you around until you get your ears dry. When I told the preacher I would take charge of this, I didn't know we were going to be in harvest, though. Darndest thing you ever saw. We just got these hot winds and turned her ripe about a week faster than everybody thought, and she all turned ripe at the same time too. But we'll get her. We always do. Those your bags?"

The question caught K.D. by surprise. It was the first thing in that whole speech that he had understood, and he was still caught trying to make meaning somewhere in the middle. So Charlie repeated the question, but impatiently this time, "Those your bags over there?"

This time K.D. seized the opportunity to jump in when he had the chance. "Yes."

"Well, that old wreck over there is my pickup. We'll load those bags in the old pickup and I'll take you to the widow woman's where you'll be staying. As I was saying, it's kind of too bad in a way you had to come in the middle of harvest when everybody is so busy." As he was talking, Charlie walked over and picked up the bag filled with the commentaries and study Bibles. He dropped it immediately and went on with his same sounds. "What in the world kind of clothes you got in there anyway? A steel suit?"

"Those are books." K.D. thought he said it with dignity but he was so shocked by all the events that he couldn't tell for sure.

"Oh, you are one of them preachers that reads a lot of books, eh? Well, I ain't much for books myself. I guess they are all right. But I am a quiet guy myself. I spend a lot of time just listening. That's the way you really get to know things. Just listen to people talk, I always say. You load the books. I'll load the clothes."

K.D. obeyed, and when everything was loaded, he followed the motion and got in himself. This was a new experience. K.D. had never been in a pickup truck before, and this one didn't look much like those in the commercials he had seen on T.V. It was cluttered with wrenches, bolts, ropes, and farm paraphernalia K.D. couldn't recognize. And dirt covered everything the junk didn't. The only clean spot was the outline of Charlie's body on his side of the seat. K.D. tried to brush himself a clean spot without trying to look conspicuous, but decided it was futile and climbed into the dirt, suit and all.

During this, Charlie kept talking. K.D. listened, interpreting as much as he could.

"Like I was saying, you just got to understand harvest around here. This is our big time. We work out there in those fields all year for a couple of weeks in June. We either make it now or we live on black-eyed peas and pig fat the rest of the year. Well, I guess it's a lot like an invitation to you preachers. You can preach all day long if you want to, but it don't do no good until you stop and cut what you sowed. Ever notice how hard preachers work during an invitation? They just get plumb lively, some of them do. That's the way we are at harvest. Out there working."

"If this is the busy season, why is the town so deserted?" K.D. didn't really mean to ask that question, not out loud at least, but he was so surprised to find a break in the flow that he said the first thing that came to him.

"That's what I've been trying to tell you. They're all out in the harvest somewhere. It takes nearly everybody running the combines, driving trucks, working in the elevator, cooking the meals, running errands, fixing the breakdowns. Where you from, Boy?"

K.D. wanted to bristle at that. He wasn't a boy. He was K.D. Garrett, pastor of the First Baptist Church, for nine weeks at least, and this man had to understand that. But when he looked back over at this stranger named Charlie, he saw more friendship than he expected—something about the structure of the face. It wasn't the eyes, because his hat was pulled down over his eyes in such a way K.D. couldn't see them, but that sun-baked skin, wrinkled by smiles and laughter, gave off a feeling of hospitality which K.D. couldn't ignore, particularly when Charlie represented about the only sign of the human race he had seen since he got off the bus. "Tulsa," K.D. said with a tone which he hoped sounded friendly.

"Tulsa, eh? I have an aunt living in Tulsa. Her name is the same as mine, Brady. Bernice really, but we call her Bertie, Bertie Brady." He paused and looked over at K.D. as if he were expecting some sign of recognition. When he didn't see any, he went on as if he were encouraging a memory or at least a spark.

"Older woman, in her eighties, maybe even ninety by now. She used to be about medium height, but old age has shrunk her up pretty good." He paused and looked at K.D. again, but K.D. only stared ahead. Charlie tried even harder. "Well, she lives off down there by that television preacher's outfit, that healer."

Since the last part trailed into a question, K.D. saw his opportunity both to say something and to add a piece of information, "Oral Roberts."

"Yeah," Charlie said, relieved. "He's the one. You know her then?" He looked toward K.D. grinning.

"No." K.D. tried to pause while he regrouped from the snare.

"No. I just know where Oral Roberts University is on the south side of Tulsa. No. I don't know your aunt." But right then, he wished he did.

"Oh," Charlie said, as if he had just confirmed his suspicion that all city people are isolated, lonely, and stuck up. But he went on anyway as if he saw his chance to correct this flaw in at least one person from the city. "Bertie married my daddy's younger brother, John, and they went over to Tulsa during the dust bowl days. Everybody thought that was a little strange. Everyone else was going west to California, but not those two. They went east and got jobs. Old John made a killing during the war selling. . . . " Somewhere between Charlie's mouth and K.D.'s brain, the heat demolished the sound waves and K.D. couldn't hear anymore, so he looked instead. The town was flat and square. To get to their destination, they went straight east, then north. For the most part, the town was filled with white frame houses which looked like they were occupied by someone named Bertie Brady. But right in the middle of a whole block of those simple houses would stand a near mansion, built of native stone, sprawling across two lots, and featuring a two- or three-car attached garage with a wide concrete driveway, stained red by the dirt that had dropped from parked vehicles. K.D. marveled at the paradox and tried to draw an analogy from it, but they came to a stop too soon.

As if to offer one final piece of manly advice, Charlie accented the stop by saying, "Careful about this widow woman. She gets kind of lonely and she just may talk your leg off before the summer is over."

K.D. wondered if he should laugh or say, "Thanks," but Charlie bounced out of the pickup before he had a chance to make a choice.

Together, they stepped around a tall bordering hedge which surrounded the yard and started up the sidewalk when they spotted someone on the porch painting. It was Mrs. Strommer. She was a short woman, tiny in the shoulders but heavier in the hips and legs. She had on a long-sleeved blue chambray shirt and an old pair of blue overalls which were too big and too long. Although she had rolled the legs up several times, she still couldn't keep from stepping on the cuffs. She stood on a kitchen step stool and painted the ceiling of the porch just above the swing. She worked with fast strokes and quick movements and obvious concentration and did not hear K.D. and Charlie approach until they were on the second step.

When she became conscious of their presence, she turned around and stared for a moment; then went back to her painting, but she started talking as she did. "Well, there's the new preacher. Right on time too. I like that in a person, prompt. Means you're neat. You look just like I thought you would, maybe a little stuffier but other than that. . . . Now, Charlie Brady, don't you dare ask me what I am doing here. That board up above the swing has rotted plumb out. Paint's cheaper than wood. You should know that, Charlie; you lived through the depression too."

With that, she gave the board one final splat and descended the ladder while taking up a new line of chatter. Charlie stood at one side, silent and polite. "Follow me. That old room down in the basement has a door that opens to the backyard. This hot sun may be the ticket for wheat farmers, but it sure ain't much good for vegetables. Just look at those potato vines. Drying up already. Watch your step there. I watered this morning, but I can't do that again. Water just costs too much. Ain't that funny? Water is supposed to be free, just like salvation, but it sure costs a lot to get it piped to you. Don't bump your head on the beam there." And she led them down five basement steps into a neat, cool room with dark maple walls and throw rugs scattered thick over the floor. The furniture was not antique, but old. The dresser and nightstand built out of dark-stained wood seemed sturdy enough to last forever. The bed was a 1930 model with huge wooden posters and thick springs and mattress which put the surface up so high that K.D. would have to climb just to get into bed. Covered in a black-and-white checkered spread, the bed looked cool and inviting, like an oasis.

As K.D. surveyed the room with more satisfaction than he had enjoyed all day, Charlie stood aside silently, and Mrs. Strommer kept talking. "I told you this room is nice. Cool down here all summer long. My husband used to come down here and take naps in the middle of the afternoon. In fact, he died right here in this room. Over there in the bed. Came down one hot summer afternoon to take a nap and just died in the bed. No sign of struggle or anything, so he must have went just like that. Never suffered once. That was eight years ago now. We had really only just lived here less than ten years then. Moved in from the farm, you know. Sometimes these old farmers don't live too long when you take them away from those chickens and cows and make them come to town. I changed the sheets for you. What is your name again?"

"K.D. Garrett." Those weren't the words he wanted to say, and he said them quieter than he intended, but he hadn't heard his own voice for so long and he had been rushed through so many emotions that he had to reacclimate to the world outside his mind before he could get coherent again.

But as it turned out, it didn't matter how he said them. "Well, young man, I hope you enjoy this room. I don't tolerate liquor or smoking, never have. Of course, you being a preacher, I guess that isn't a problem. Other than that, just make yourself to home. You need to get your rest; you've got a busy summer ahead of you. A lot of learning to do, but you are going to do us some good too. At least, we all hope you do."

She continued to talk, as Charlie and K.D. carried in the bags. When they had finished, Charlie went back to the pickup as fast as he could. K.D. Garrett stood halfway between Mrs. Strommer and Charlie looking for a spot to say good-bye to her, but when he couldn't find it, he just waved and climbed back through the dust and tools on his side of the vehicle. Mrs. Strommer stooped in the garden and began picking weeds.

Charlie started before the truck did. "Her old man was a real corker. During the thirties when times was so hard, he moved the whole family out of their house—wasn't much of a house, just a three room shack—but he just moved everybody to the cellar. Said it saved fuel. Lived there almost a year, as best as I can remember. She's a tough old gal, that one, but she comes by it natural."

By then, they had driven west two blocks and had come up to the back side of the steep-roofed, white frame building which K.D. had already recognized as the First Baptist Church. The yard was bare and the building was old, but it was better kept than K.D. had earlier thought. Up close, it looked like a building that someone cared about. The walls were freshly painted, the eaves had been repaired, and the big, arched stained-glass windows, one in the south wall and another in the north, had obviously been made by an artisan. A little white house which looked like all the other town houses stood off at the northeast corner and was connected to the main building by an enclosed passageway.

As the men came to the church, K.D. looked and Charlie provided the travelogue. With ample illustrations from the past, he explained that the attached house was not the parsonage anymore but served as offices and Sunday School rooms. The rest of the Sunday School rooms and the kitchen were in the basement, except that one class of the older people met up in the church itself. They had a room for them downstairs, but they were too bullheaded to use it, and they were too old to argue with, so everybody just left them alone.

The tour and the stories culminated in the sanctuary itself. As K.D. stood and surveyed the place where he would cut his teeth on the cloth, and realized that he had never been in a Baptist Church this old before, he felt like somebody out of a Hawthorne short story. All the woodwork was dark mahogany, which was set off by red cushions on the pews and red carpet up and down the aisles. The pews were arranged in a semicircle with a curved set in the middle and two short sets along each wing. The podium was high, almost three steps up. The pulpit was large and the top was covered with red velvet, except for the face of the electric clock which showed through. Red drapes covered the face of the baptistry. Just above it someone had cut through the dark mahogany backdrop to install the face of a large water-cooled squirrel-cage fan.

As K.D. checked the main features and the crevices, Charlie answered some of his questions without meaning to. "Lots of other towns around here have brand new churches. Long and lean. Cinder blocks and carpet on the floor. Windows all up and down and all the wood stained light. When they first started building them, they looked pretty enough, but after a while they all looked alike. Well, some here talked about building a new church a few years back, but we just didn't do it. That ain't the kind of people we are in Wheatheart. Other towns are all trying to figure out who they are. But we already know and we aren't ashamed of it. We just don't do things because that is the way everyone else is doing them. You'll find us a little more stable than that."

From there, Charlie moved the tour through the passageway into the pastor's office, explaining that the secretary would be off for two weeks. She always gets harvest off and takes her vacation whenever they start to cut wheat. Finally, Charlie led the way into the pastor's office where he said that K.D. could hide out for the next nine weeks. The office itself was large enough and rather well constructed, but it was decorated in kid's art, illustrated Bible verses and some Christian trinkets. The few books on the shelves were crowded into corners without any hint of a system. K.D. glanced only briefly, but saw nothing significant. He wasn't surprised.

From the church, they drove down Main Street past the other church, which turned out to be Methodist, past the drugstore, across the Highway, past the Dew Drop Inn and parked in front of the green and yellow of the John Deere store. Charlie sat at the steering wheel and finished a story before he announced, "I'm going to let you out here. Scott Garland is going to provide you with a car to drive. You just go in and ask for him. He owns the place. "I've got to get back out to the wheat field. I don't do all that much, but I run the combines to let the boys off for supper. You'll get along all right—I'll catch you later after I get this harvest out of the way."

And with that, K.D.'s mysterious friend whipped his pickup into a huge U-turn and headed back up Main Street, leaving him stranded on the curb outside the John Deere store. The yard was filled with implements and gadgets which he couldn't name, but there was a certain sense of disheveled prosperity to all the clutter. The number of pickups parked along the curb indicated a good business.

When he got inside, what he saw was more like a flea market than a legitimate business. Men in overalls covered with grease and straw stood belly-up to a chest high counter, carefully inspecting iron pieces as if they were made of precious stone. Behind the counter, the clerks ran from bin to bin and shelf to shelf hunting for the next piece as if they were in a race with all the other clerks to get their orders filled first.

K.D. walked up to the counter, flagged the first running clerk and asked simply, "Scott Garland?" The clerk didn't even slow down; he just pointed to a man back by a bin and kept running. K.D. walked over nearer and called across the counter, "Mr. Garland?"

The man looked up from his search for the right bolt from a bin full of assorted bolts. "Oh, I'll bet you're the new Baptist preacher." K.D. was pleased that it showed this late in the afternooon. The man went on. "I just want you to know that I'm behind you 1000 percent. Anything you want, you just name it. My wife goes more regularly than I do, but I am still a big supporter, so just tell me what you need."

K.D. felt better than he had felt all day long. This was a man who was obviously sincere about his religious convictions. He was not a chronic gossiper and he seemed intelligent. "At least," K.D. thought, "I am going to have one friend." With that attitude, he thanked Scott for the offer with the same sincerity with which the offer had been made; as he did, the man kept one eye on his search and one eye on K.D. But that was all right. K.D. understood.

Scott excused himself for the busyness and said, "You probably came after your vehicle. Well, it's that old white Chevy pickup parked outside. The keys are in it. You just go get it and drive it like it's yours." And with that, Scott went back to searching intensely, and K.D. went out to find the old white Chevy pickup.

This was some turn of events for him. Less that two hours ago, he had ridden in a pickup for the first time in his life, and now he was even going to drive one. So far, the place had about met all his expectations. He knew it was going to be primitive and different—

the town, the church and even the room—but in all his dreading, he had never thought to dread having to drive a pickup truck. Not only had K.D. never driven a pickup truck, but he had never known any minister who had.

As he opened the door to the old white Chevy, he saw that this truck was just as dirty as Charlie's, but without the junk. He brushed the seat off as best he could and slid in under the wheel where he paused to get the feel of things. Some of the equipment was in normal places, the horn, light switch, windshield wipers; and with a bit of a search, he found other familiar necessities such as the brake and the accelerator. But then he discovered what wasn't familiar—the gearshift and to his dismay, the clutch. The pickup was a stick shift. K.D. had never driven a stick shift. He had seen people shift and he thought he knew the procedure, but he had never done it himself.

But here he was stuck in the south end of Main Street in the middle of an equipment yard with no way to get out but to make the clutch and shift work.

Timidly, he started the engine and waited as he built up his nerve and checked to see if any one from inside was watching.

Then he pushed in the pedal and found first gear with the lever. So far, so good. Again, he waited, holding the pedal in, almost afraid to let it out; but as he withdrew his foot, the motor died. He checked again to make sure he was alone, and tried it once more. This time, he lifted his foot more slowly, but that wasn't the answer, since the motor died again. After another check for an audience, he started the engine again. This time, he pushed in the accelerator until the engine was racing.

He thought he took his foot off the clutch slowly, but the pickup jerked forward with a snap, wrenching his back and throwing his stomach against the steering wheel where it marked a deep red dirt stain across his light blue jacket. The fourth time, he managed to coordinate the clutch and accelerator enough to get the vehicle moving and he navigated through the machinery and out into the middle of Main Street without a major hitch. Very slowly, he drove up Main Street in this one gear until he was comfortable with the operation.

Somewhere about in front of the Dew Drop Inn, he decided to try shifting. He pushed in the clutch pedal, pulled the shift lever into second, and took his foot off the clutch. The pickup bolted forward, screeching the tires. K.D., frightened by the noise, crammed the brakes down and the tires screeched again as the pickup came to a halt. K.D. had only a moment to suffer panic because another emotion came hard on its heels, embarrassment. Human forms rushed to the windows and door stoops of every store on both sides of Main Street. The grain trucks parked along both sides of Main Street each burped at least one driver who rushed to the corners of their trucks, stood, stared, and snickered. Men who had moved those massive machines into those tight spaces laughed at the character in the suit and tie who was trying to drive this pickup down Main Street. K.D.'s first impulse was to get out, slam the door, and storm away—but it was an impulse which had brought him here in the first place. Now he would never trust his impulses again. With no other options available, he put the machine back in first gear, drove up Main Street, until he found a side street which looked vacant. Then he wound his way to the edge of town and onto a country road.

When he was well enough away from the population, where no other human could see or hear, he practiced his driving. He didn't perfect the art that night, but he stayed out on the country roads until he got good enough to shift on Main Street.

If he had not been so busy with his own problems, he might have seen the cemetery or the hills up along the road nine miles north, or the rock peaks west of town, or a sunset that stretched across a thousand miles of western horizon. Or he might have noticed the activities of harvest, men and machines working in harmony to gather the grain before hail, or wind, or insects beat them to it. But he didn't see any of that. Rather he felt his frustrations, and his anger, and his loneliness and wished he were somewhere else.

When dusk and some proficiency at shifting reminded him that it was time to go home, he discovered the lights of the town, and drove toward them until he found his way to Mrs. Strommer's house. He heard her talking to someone on the front porch swing, so he crept beside the house and tiptoed down to the quiet of the basement room. The room was as comfortable in the night time as it had been in the day, so he quickly slipped out of his clothes, refreshed himself with a shower, snacked on some crackers and cookies Rebecca had sent along, celebrated the security of privacy, and consoled himself with letter-writing.

Notes From Siberia

Dear Rebecca,

The world has its Byrd, its Columbus, its Stanley, and now its Garrett. I have discovered the best-kept secret of the modern age, a hot Siberia. I have even answered the question which puzzled the pre-Socratic philosophers. All atoms are made out of red dirt. In Wheatheart there is no human life, only harvest.

After one afternoon, my suit is soiled beyond hope and my soul is weary. The town itself is propped up with old boards. Everywhere and everything has more of a past than a present or a future—nothing new, nothing young, nothing alive with hope. Even the church lives out of the dust bowl of the thirties, reminding these people that living is suffering. As I write these words, I lie on the very bed where Mr. Strommer died, and it is the most refreshing spot I have found.

So far, I have met a total of three people. My host, who rode into town out of an early John Wayne movie, personifies the activity of oral history. I have never met anybody who talks more than he does, except for Mrs. Strommer. But where he just relives without commentary or malice, she cuts and digs and pries.

On the other hand, Mr. Garland, the leading businessman, who sells tractors, seems to be quick-witted and supportive with a distinctive Christian flair, a possibility for a friendship if I decide to stay past the week.

You know me. I am not an elitist. On the contrary, I am but a common man, but I shall never fit in here. There is a code which I shall never learn.

In an earlier time, I was competent and, even at times, skillful. Caught in this country conspiracy, I am worse than worthless. I feel I am the laughing goat, let loose here to carry for them the sins of the town. Adroitly, I have navigated the Tulsa streets, and have even served as guide and narrator. By skillful thinking, I adjusted to Fort Worth. Once I even drove through Dallas traffic to the Texas-Oklahoma football game, but today I amused the natives when I could not propel a primitive vehicle up Main Street.

This is degradation rather than education. It is destruction rather than growth.

I miss you. Even in this heat, I miss your warmth, your smile, your cleanliness, and your gentle hand. I have nothing to remind me of what I have ever been before, and what I am now is of no value. So I am worthless. I am here now, but I am not sure I am planning to stay.

I must talk to someone about something of importance or shall I go mad.

With deep fondness,
K.D.

A New Language

The next morning K.D. Garrett, pastor of the First Baptist Church, awoke early, surprised to find that he had slept well. After some debate with himself, he chose for the day's costume a short-sleeved dress shirt, sans the jacket, but he did tie and retie his tie four times before he got both the knot and the length exactly right.

Just before walking up the basement steps and stepping out into his parish, he studied his image in the old dresser mirror which was clouded by age. He did not like his dress style; it was more confused than official, but he was not going to ruin another jacket today. But after studying the total picture for a moment, he glanced at the image of his face and was almost shocked at how young he looked. The picture frightened him, so he hurried on about his duties before he had a chance to dwell on the significance.

He first thought he would drive the pickup down to the Dew Drop Inn for breakfast, but a combination of remembering yesterday's experience with the pickup on Main Street and the calmness of the early morning persuaded him to walk instead. After all, it was only a few blocks.

Although the sun was just rising over the eastern prairie, he could tell that it would be another bright day. The sky was solid blue from horizon to horizon without even so much as a hint of a cloud. Already, it was more comfortable walking in the shade than standing in the direct sunlight. Even this early in the morning, the air was filled with the stench of new-cut wheat. Although the elevator din had died out somewhere through the night, there was still the sense of urgency. Something was about to erupt again. Too soon, people throughout all the area would be scampering about their business like characters in an old film. The red dirt was not really gone but hiding, lurking in the early morning mist, waiting to spring out and attack.

This early in the morning, the houses looked empty, with little evidence of life yet, except that somewhere at nearly each house, on the porch, in the driveway, or the sunniest part of the yard, someone had already placed the huge jar filled with cool water and tea bags.

Throughout the whole trip across the side street and down Main Street, K.D. saw only two moving vehicles, pickups, the basic equipment of the local industry, and both times the people in the pickups stared at him, even turning their necks as they passed by to stare even harder and more judgmentally.

The Dew Drop Inn itself was filled with activity and urgency. The Cafe was no cleaner than K.D. had expected. The decor was early dinette. Assorted tables and unmatched chairs were scattered about with no apparent scheme. Four booths lined one wall, but they too looked disorganized. Men, and only men, sat around the tables and booths at random, hunkered over plates of food, eating with quick movements and big bites. Between bites, with their mouths only fractionally full, they would inject a comment into the group conversation.

"I can't believe that made sixty bushels."

"That's what he said?"

"The whole quarter made sixty bushels?"

"I had some made fifty-five, but it was only a patch, a bottom terrace."

"No breakdowns yet, knock on wood," and he knocked on the

formica table top.

"Elevator lines aren't all that bad."

"Having a lift on the truck instead of using theirs sure helps."

"Speaking of lifts, did you hear about that kid over by Alva?"

"Yeah, cut his head off."

"Lifted up the bed and leaned inside to grease it."

"The whole bed fell on him and cut his head right off."

"I carry a stick just for that purpose."

"Yeah, but we get in a hurry during harvest."

"Take a lot of dumb chances."

"Well, if you ask me, just sowing it is the biggest chance of all."

"Ain't that the truth! What was it yesterday?"

"Three bucks and fifteen."

"Can't make money doing that."

"Gotta run. Maybe some of mine'll make seventy today."

"Don't take any wooden nickels."

"Did you hear about that kid up at Alva?"

"Cut his head off greasing the lift."

The conversation was corporate and perpetual. Participants would leave and new ones would enter to take their places. As best as K.D. could tell, it didn't matter where you came in. There seemed to be no apparent beginning, middle, or end. But since it was all a new language to him, K.D. couldn't tell for sure what was going on. When newcomers came, no one greeted them or called their names and no one said good-bye.

K.D. moved through the maze of tables, took one of the six chairs at the counter, and waited until the one busy waitress could get to him. As she carried plates of food up and down both arms, her gait was almost a lope. Although it was only shortly after seven A.M., she looked as if she had been working forever. She carried a towel around her neck and when she paused at a table with pen and pad ready to write down an order, she would wipe away the perspiration.

Without saying a word, she brought K.D. coffee and water and stood with pen and pad until he ordered. She brought his food and his check at the same time and moved off again without speaking a word.

The whole atmosphere frightened and bored K.D. These people were too serious about something he knew nothing about. As best he could tell, in biblical language, they were straining at gnats. They talked but weren't friendly.

Although the food was suprisingly wholesome and plentiful, K. D. ate quickly. He wanted to get away as fast as he could. But as he leaned over to the cash register on the countertop to pay his bill to the rushing waitress, he said to her softly but with as much dignity as he could muster in those surroundings, "I'm Pastor Garrett of the First Baptist Church."

She didn't break stride, either in her face or her actions. She made change and without looking up said, "Yeah, I knew you were a preacher. Nobody else in his right mind would get all dressed up unless he had to." She plopped the money into K.D.'s hand and started loading her arms with plates of food.

K.D. walked back up Main Street toward the church and tried to think. But he couldn't make his mind think about what it should think about. Instead, he thought about Fort Worth, the seminary, the professors, the conversations around the dining hall table, and about Rebecca. Through random thoughts instead of disciplined ones, that part of the day became at least bearable.

Once at the church, K.D. went directly to Brother Bob's office, his office now, and remembered that he was glad the secretary was gone and he could be alone here. He pulled a very worn King James Bible from the shelf and browsed through it, feasting on the under-lined verses and the margin notes, scribbled in all colors, some looking fresh and others faded. After several minutes of this, K.D. felt like worshiping, so he put the Bible under his arm and walked back through the passageway into the sanctuary. Although the room was really too dark to do too much reading, K.D. found a spot in one of the middle pews where the early morning sunlight filtered through the stained glass windows and made a prism on everything there to receive the hues. After adjusting himself into the right light,

K.D. opened the Bible and read from the Psalms. Wherever he turned, the plots were the same. Desperation, despair, defeat, and then the glory of God shining through, breaking the chains and brightening the day. That refreshed K.D. and he wished he could sit in that spot forever. When he checked his watch, he realized that he almost had. It was already past ten, and he had things to do. With a burst of enthusiasm unlike anything he had experienced since he had stepped on that bus in Fort Worth, yesterday or years ago, he couldn't remember which, he walked back down Main Street. After all, this was his town. He was the pastor here. He needed to serve these people; and to do that, he had to get acquainted with them.

That enthusiasm carried him into nearly every store up and down Main Street until he was drained completely, and this time cut deeper than he had been before, because the enthusiasm had made him tender, more vulnerable. No one was friendly. The people in the stores, usually only one, spoke to him when they thought he was a customer; but when he introduced himself as Pastor Garrett, they hurried on about their duties. A few shook his outstretched hand, but some didn't do that. What hurt K.D. worst was that there was no reason behind the urgency. There were no customers. Oh, there were a couple of older ladies buying groceries at the Red Bud, and someone was making a deposit at one of the banks, but other than that, there were no customers.

The people in the stores were redecorating, cleaning, shuffling, and acting as if it had to be done today. K.D. could see the need. Most of the places looked as if they could stand some cleaning and updating, but he couldn't see the urgency. This was work which needed to have been done weeks ago, but why just now?

Since he could see no reasons, he drew only one conclusion; the town was unfriendly, not just to him but to everybody. These people were in too big a hurry chasing nothing to spend time thinking about anyone else except themselves. Like the breakfast conversation, they were in a hurry to get to nowhere. If he could have asked someone, he would have discovered that this too was the spirit of harvest. The whole town was in a hurry. The people on the farms hurried to get the wheat in, and the people in town hurried because they wanted to have the cleaning and decorating finished when harvest was over. But no one explained it to him because no one thought that their activity or attitude was unusual.

Rather depressed by it all, K.D. found at least a pleasant memory in the letter he needed to mail, and so he walked over to the post office. Like all the other places of business, the clerk was almost too busy to sell him a stamp; but when he stepped around the corner into the mailbox section, he came face to face with a pleasant looking man standing right in the middle of the floor casually reading his mail. He was not really a big man, but something about him, maybe pride, made him seem bigger than he was. His eyes, deep-set behind heavy brows, were bright and intense. He was casually but tastefully dressed, in a sport shirt and old khakis. He looked like someone's father and maybe everybody's father.

K.D. drew up his courage, tried to remember his earlier enthusiasm and dared take one more chance at friendliness. "I'm Pastor Garrett of the First Baptist Church," he said and extended his hand.

The man enveloped K.D.'s hand in his, did a year's research with those intense eyes, and said, "I'm Coach Rose."

K.D. smiled, and for the first time all day, it was sincere. "I'm sorry, I didn't get the first name."

"Coach," the man said gently.

At that moment, K.D. couldn't tell whether he should be embarrassed or accepting of that answer, but his attempt to cover his confusion was awkward. "Oh, coach of what?" he asked, because he couldn't think of anything else.

The man still looked pleasant. "I'm the high school football coach here."

This time K.D. was surprised. "I didn't realize Wheatheart had a football team," and he tried to imagine it based on what he had seen so far.

"Oh, yes," Coach Rose said, as if he sensed that K.D. was embarrassed.

K.D. struggled for a new direction because he wanted to keep the conversation alive. "Are you very good?" That was a silly question. Although he wasn't that much of an athlete himself, he knew enough about sports not to ask that.

Coach Rose tried to be kind, but he, too, was disturbed with the question. "Well, we won the state last year."

Now K.D. was both embarrassed and impressed. Why didn't he know this? "Wow, that's fantastic. That must have been some thrill."

Now Coach Rose was embarrassed. "Maybe not as much as it should have been. We've won the state six times out of the last twelve years."

Since both men were struggling at this point, K.D. decided to try the virtue of apology. "I'm sorry to be so ignorant. I should have heard of you people. Winning the state that many times!"

That seemed to ease Coach Rose, and he said simply, "No need to apologize. Winning the state in football is not really memorable news except in the town where it happens." But as he said that, he had a look in his face as if he understood what it meant.

K.D. saw that look and was encouraged by it. He checked his spiritual equipment, remembered his four spiritual laws, and decided to try to be a pastor. "Tell me, Coach, are you a man of God?"

Coach Rose, still relaxed and pleasant, looked at K.D. through those eyes which saw more than they revealed, and said, "Only on a personal basis."

At that moment, K.D. cursed his seminary education for being inadequate. For that answer, he had no words. Only a blank stare like a child in a play who has forgotten his lines. Finally, he sensed that it was time to go. He reached out his hand, felt it engulfed again, and said "I just want you to know, Coach, that you are welcome at any service of the First Baptist Church."

The coach was gracious and sincere. "Why thank you. That's kind of you." And with the same graciousness and sincerity, he said, "And I want you to know that you are welcome at any football practice at Wheatheart." With that, he turned and walked out the door.

Finally, when he had found a friendly face after a full day of searching, the new pastor had been bested and he knew it. He went home to his monk's cell, like a puppy with his tail between his legs. He didn't like this town, and now he didn't like himself.

Teleological Proofs

The next day, K.D. moved his books from the cases in his room into his study at the church. Except for breakfast, which went like the day before, and a brief lunch snack at the Whippet Drive Inn where he didn't have to listen to customer talk, he worked at making the study his. For most of the day, he managed to avoid Mrs. Strommer, getting caught only twice and losing thirty minutes both times. But it was through the conversations with Mrs. Strommer that he found his direction for the week. Both times he encountered her, she talked about Brother Bob's sermons, some recent and some from distant past. She even remembered word for word the sermon he had preached at her husband's funeral, or at least she remembered the words she would have preached had she been Brother Bob.

Through the day, as K.D. would remember those secondhand sermons, he suddenly realized that maybe he had misinterpreted his call here. Maybe these people really didn't need a pastor, a shepherd. They didn't even have time for conversation, much less his personal ministry to them, and everyone seemed so independent and self-sufficient. Maybe what they needed was a good sermon every Sunday. And that thought pleased him. Now he could do his scholarship and fulfill his mission. He would just direct his efforts toward preaching.

With that, he threw himself into his ministry for the rest of the week. For his text he selected Psalm 104, and for a title he chose, "The Teleological Proofs of God." Since Mrs. Strommer hadn't quoted a sermon like that, he felt it could be an unexplored field for them.

He spent hours in the study with his Bible and other books, skipping meals and staying late into the night. He reread Augustine, Luther, and Calvin. He searched for and found sermon illustrations in books of nature, in such stories as the swallows at Capistrano and the suicide march of the lemmings in Norway. He found other illustrations in Scripture such as Christ directing the fishermen to great schools of fish. When he had gathered all the information in order, he stretched it out across his desk, and put together an outline.

Introduction: Look around you and see order and purpose
  I. There is order and purpose
     A. The world is intelligible
     B. The inorganic world is perfectly suited to sustain life
     C. There is an odd and overwhelming beauty in nature
     D. There is a universal moral sense and political organiza-
        tion in all colonies of the human race
 II. The world has a designer
     A. Fate or chance can not produce inherent order or beauty
     B. The world is like a watch, intricately designed, but
        even more so (the quote from William Paley)
III. God is the designer
     A. The order of creation (Psalm 104:10-26)
     B. God is in complete control (Psalm 104:27-30)

It was a good outline, solid, well thought out, all points documented, and it had potential in delivery.

Fortunately, K.D. completed the outline late Friday night, which gave him time to spend all day Saturday on delivery. He worked on gestures and accents. He even went into the sanctuary and stood behind the pulpit with the red cushion and the clock staring in his face, and he imagined a church full of people. Using what little physics of sound he remembered from a college course, he ascertained where the dead spots might be and planned strategies for ways to reach them too. With this sermon, no one would miss a single point.

He typed his notes clearly on the pica typewriter in the office; but just in case, he committed them all to memory. He was excited when he called his parents from the church office Saturday afternoon. Without too much effort, he sounded pleasant and even, at times, optimistic. This was going to be a good summer. He had a nice room, good food, and an opportunity to preach from his knowledge.

Although his mother was not as anxious as she had been before, she still had plenty of advice about safe driving tips and staying out of the hot sun. He listened patiently, and chuckled to himself as he thought of the sermon notes tucked into his Bible and committed to memory.

Late Saturday night, in the sanctuary of his basement room, he stood in front of the clouded dresser mirror and practiced reading the text. Over and over again he practiced.

Then he climbed up into the bed and waited fitfully for Sunday morning to come, kept awake by the anticipation of just one more step to complete in having done a job well.

7

The Wheatheart Flock

Sunday morning was beautiful. Although the air still smelled of newly cut wheat, and the elevator din started before the Sunday School hour, there was a calm through the town which said that this was Sunday. Everyone felt it, and especially K.D. as he walked up to the office early in the morning, dressed in a new three-piece beige suit with a brown handkerchief in his pocket.

He chose not to go to Sunday School. His mind was too full to meet anyone just then. He would stay in his office and make his entrance at the beginning of church. There would be time later for introductions, at the door after the service when people would have something to say to him.

He sat calmly at his desk and tried vainly to divert his attention to his own private devotions. He checked his pulse and found it was ten beats per minute faster than normal. He knew he was ready; he had prepared. Now he prayed for God's blessing on what he had done and was yet to do.

After what seemed like more than a month of waiting, he heard the piano play the song that told everybody that it was time to finish their conversations and come into the house of worship. He gathered a large Bible under his arm and walked through the passageway into the sanctuary to face the crowd. In one glance he counted them, sixteen people scattered all over the auditorium. Mrs. Strommer and five other women about her age, an elderly couple who both wore hearing aids, four middle-aged women and four children under school age.

Since Mrs. Strommer was sitting in a conspicuous spot on the front row, K.D. could get to her easily as he made his way to the pulpit, so he stopped and whispered, "Do you think this will be the crowd?" He tried not to show his disappointment.

Instead of whispering, she answered out loud, "Sure, right in the middle of harvest like this. In fact, more here than I thought there would be. Yes, I think this is everybody."

During the song service, K.D. mouthed the words without hearing or remembering what he sang. Somehow he managed the ritual of taking an offering by using one middle-aged woman and the elderly man.

And then he stepped to the pulpit and delivered his sermon on "The Teleological Proofs of God." By now this sermon was a part of him. The points came to mind without his thinking about them. The gestures and accents were appropriate in place and time, and the words flowed smoothly. In his dreams, K.D. stood before the congregation of the First Baptist Church of Dallas, and delivered one of the finest sermons they had ever heard—informative, persuasive and provocative. Although he went past twelve by more than six minutes, the material warranted it and everyone forgave him as he finished in a flourish.

Back to reality, K.D. stepped to the rear of the church and greeted his flock. Everyone stopped to chat, and to thank him for coming to Wheatheart to be their preacher for the summer. One woman once knew someone named Garrett and wondered if he was a relative; others knew people from Tulsa; one lady even had a distant nephew at the seminary in Fort Worth, but she couldn't remember his name. No one commented about the message, except Mrs. Strommer, who said in her matter-of-fact way, "I didn't get a thing out of that sermon, but it is good to be in church anyway."

Since harvest had called off the evening service, K.D. could devote the whole afternoon to writing letters and reading.

Notes From Solitary

That Sunday afternoooon, the tiny basement room protected K.D. Garrett from the hot winds and the activity of the community outside.

With no other minds around, he interacted with people in his books—Calvin, Wesley, Spurgeon, and Augustine. Idea by idea, sentence by sentence, and even word by word, he debated and applauded the great minds who had thought about the things he enjoyed thinking about; and in that forum he created for himself, he forgot about broken awnings, the Dew Drop Inn Cafe, Wheatheart, and harvest.

When pleasantness came back to his being, he wrote to Rebecca. In the beginning and throughout most of the letter, he did not mention Wheatheart because he wasn't even thinking about it.

With the Rebecca he created from his memory sitting beside him in the room, he discussed great ideas including the teleological proofs of God. He wrote his appreciation for the scholars—Augustine, Calvin, Wesley, Spurgeon, and even Casper. He looked into his future and a time when he would take his place among them.

But eventually, when his mind brought him back to the present and the reality of the day, his mood changed. Although there was no one present to see it, his facial expression altered. Not knowing what else to do with his new mood, he wrote on.

Notes From Solitary Confinement

Send help quick. Crucifixion is the only suffering I have not yet met, and now that sounds welcome. I don't believe the emotions which have found their way into my being, and I can't always identify them. I don't know the difference between anger and frustration, and I don't know how to keep anger from turning to hate.

These are God's people. This is God's world too. Is it by mutual consent that they ignore each other?

I want to instruct; I want to be used; I want my life to stand for something; but here I am worthless, preaching well for people who don't know the difference. What's the use of knowing, of studying, if you can't help another to understand?

And the wound is deep today because the hope was so high only yesterday. My sermon was an A plus in homiletics class anywhere, and only sixteen people could leave their own activity long enough to hear it.

Now I am confused. Shall I continue to prepare fine sermons, ageless sermons, in the event that God gives me the opportunity at another place and another time? Shall I waste my time trying to serve people who don't want service? Or shall I build a shell of indifference and serve out my sentence by marking days off the calendar as they drag by?

I remember the words of the sonnet,

When in disgrace with fortune and men's eyes

I all alone beweep my outcast state,

For me the solution to the ache of loneliness is the same as it was for Shakespeare.

I think of you. I miss you. I miss your wit and understanding, your mind and intelligence, your gift for making me feel intelligent.

Please write. If for no other reason, your letter will take me to the post office, and that alone will give me cause to get out of bed this next week.

Affectionately—and lonely,
K.D.

9

Separate Worlds

Since Pastor Garrett of the First Baptist Church saw no reason to get out of bed the next morning, he didn't. He wasn't really asleep, but he wasn't fully into the real world either. He just lay there trying to remember where he was and why.

But a rap on his door stirred him out of his stupor. By the time he could get to the door, the rap had become a bang. It was Mrs. Strommer, and she had bad news. With no more introduction than that, she walked right by K.D. into his room, as if she wasn't even surprised to see her pastor still in his pajamas. As he tried to look casual, she tidied the room and dusted off the high places while she gave him the report.

"They called me this morning. They took Abe to the hospital last night. Heart Attack. Abe Ericson. Abe's still a young man, no more than forty or fifty, I would guess. But you know they lost that son. He and Mary Ruth are both such nice people. Too bad about that boy. They both took it awfully hard, and they should have. He was really a nice boy, not like some of the hooligans around here. Worked hard with his dad, wrote poetry too I think. But you know what that crazy football is good for. Just get those young boys hurt.

And now this heart attack. I don't know how bad it is, but bad enough. Any of them are. Him with all that wheat to cut and ground to plow. He must be beside himself.

"You will want to go, of course. I don't know what you can do. I don't suppose you will be much good to her in the harvest, but you can pray or do whatever it is you do to make folks feel better. They're both good people. Everybody says so. They don't mingle all that much, and Abe hasn't got that big in his farming like some people around here, but he works hard and takes care of his stuff. He's a deacon too. You'll want to go." And with that she finished the report, the commands, and the dusting, and she left.

K.D. took her advice. He dressed himself in his best-looking but still comfortable pastor's costume, reread some pages out of the minister's manual about sickbed visits, and drove the old pickup down to the hospital.

He knew it probably wasn't visiting hours, but he also knew that as a pastor he was entitled to certain privileges, and he was prepared to deal with the bureaucracy.

He didn't have to. He stopped at the front desk and told the very young looking girl in the nurse's uniform that he had come to see Mr. Ericson. He was about to explain that he was Pastor K.D. Garrett of the First Baptist Church, but she didn't give him a chance. She just told him the room number. When he wondered out loud about visiting hours, she told him that they didn't have any. "People who come here to visit," she reported, "are usually pretty busy, so we just let them go on in when they get here." With that, she went back to her work.

K.D. found the room and Abe lying in bed. Under the circumstances, K.D. could not make too many assessments about Abe, but he could tell immediately that he was not the kind of man who would ever look comfortable in a hospital bed. For one thing, the hospital gown was too small through the chest and shoulders, so Abe had the movement of being in a straitjacket; and the other indicators of Abe's profession, the deeply tanned skin and the huge hands stained by both sun and work, were out of harmony with the sterile white of the sheets and pillows.

K.D.'s first reaction was to feel sorry for Abe, even before he discovered the extent of the illness. The introductions were cordial, but more official than personal. The pastor expressed his dismay that Abe was ill, and Abe welcomed the pastor to the community. The pastor walked over to the bed, put his hand on Abe's shoulder and told him how good he looked. Abe turned away, and said under his breath that he felt good. The pastor moved the chair closer, sat down in it and asked Abe if he would like to hear some Scripture. Abe said that would be nice. The pastor read some Psalms, a passage from Corinthians, and some of the promises from the Book of Romans. Then he asked Abe if there was something special he wanted read, and Abe requested "Something about the mansions in the Father's house and the place where He is the Shepherd." Interpreting as best he could, K.D. read the first six verses of John 14 and all of Psalm 23. As he was reading, he gathered that he had interpreted correctly, because Abe lay back as comfortable as he could in all that whiteness and sterility, and somewhere inside himself found a pleasant look for his face and a quietness for his hands as he folded them over his chest.

If K.D. had only known Abe well enough, he would have understood that he found comfort not just in the text but in the familiarity of the words themselves. And if K.D. had known that about Abe, he could have understood his own emotions and feelings better, and might have known that it was all right to feel the way he did yesterday. But he couldn't know that because he couldn't know Abe very well—these two men so much alike on the inside but so different on the outside that they could not reach a common point to start a meaningful relationship.

The pastor asked about prayer requests, and Abe talked voluntarily, if not comfortably, for the first time. He wanted prayer for Mary Ruth. She was having a hard time. They had just lost a son (Abe choked on the word) and she was still trying to get over that. She didn't need anymore grief. Then they needed to pray for the crops. Abe was concerned about the crops. He still had 300 acres of ripe wheat out there, and he had no idea what was going to happen to it. Doc was usually pretty good about telling patients things, but Doc hadn't given him any hint at all. He didn't know how long he would be in the hospital, much less laid up, and they just couldn't afford to lose that 300 acres. That would send them into bankruptcy. Maybe after other farmers were finished harvesting, he could hire some help to get his wheat out, providing they didn't get a hail storm or anything. In all, Abe painted a gloomy picture.

Through courtesy, the pastor asked if Abe wanted to pray first, but Abe declined, so the pastor prayed earnestly and at length for all those things.

As K.D. walked back out into the hall, he decided he liked this man, although he surprised himself to admit it, and he committed himself to help. He could sense Abe's anxiety about the crops. If the doctor understood that anxiety, it would help Abe.

At the desk, he asked to the girl in the nursing uniform, who looked so official but had tried so hard to hide her high school blemishes, "Who is the doctor for Mr. Ericson?"

The question startled her for a moment, then she laughed more at herself than at him. "Why Doc Heimer, of course. He's the only doctor there is." By the way she declared that last sentence, K.D. couldn't tell whether she meant in Wheatheart or in the world.

"Could I speak to him?" he asked.

"Sure," she said and picked up an intercom microphone. "Doc, can you come to the waiting room please? The new preacher wants to see you." She went back to her work.

A few minutes later, the doctor wandered through the swinging doors that separated the waiting room from the rest of the hospital, walked up to K.D. and said gruffly, but rather businesslike. "Yeah? I'm Doc Heimer."

The doctor was a short, plump man who needed a shave. He wore a lab jacket which might have been clean once but never would be again. He teeth were stained, and a drop of some foreign material trickled down one corner of his mouth.

K.D. was not surprised. "I'm Pastor Garrett of the First Baptist

Church. I have come about Mr. Ericson."

"Yeah? What about him?" the doctor asked and looked over his shoulder as if he was uncomfortable.

"Well," K.D. said, "I would just like to know the extent of the damage so far." K.D. had once thought he might want to be a doctor, a medical missionary, and he had worked as an orderly and aide in a private medical center in Tulsa. He knew some of the language and procedure of a modern, scientific hospital.

Doc looked over his shoulder again, walked over to the desk, picked up an empty styrofoam cup, spat in it, returned to K.D. and said, "I don't know yet."

"So what are you planning to do?" K.D. asked impatiently.

"Wait," Doc said.

"What does the E.K.G. show?" K.D. asked, sounding rather knowledgeable.

"I didn't do one," Doc said. "Our E.K.G. machine is broken. If it becomes necessary, I'll run him over to Alva."

K.D. was shocked with that answer. He thought the E.K.G. was the beginning place for heart diagnosis. "Well, what tests have you done to determine that this man has suffered a heart attack?"

By now, Doc had cleared the tobacco from his mouth enough to talk. "We took his temperature and his blood pressure."

"So what makes you think he has had a heart attack?" K.D. asked in his best voice of incredulity.

"He's got the symptoms," Doc said with a shrug.

"But you don't know," K.D. pleaded.

"No, not for sure," and Doc spit again just by habit. "But I tell you what I do know. This man just lost a teenage son. For the first time in fifteen years, he's out there harvesting by himself. And his chest starts to hurt. He's either got a grief attack or a heart attack. I don't know which, and it really doesn't make much difference. I'm going to doctor him like he's had a heart attack, and if he has, he'll get better. If he hasn't had one, he'll get better just the same."

Then Doc changed his tone. "We sure are glad to have you in town. Good to get rid of old Brother Bob for a while. He's really kind of stuffy, you know, so it's good to have a little life here," he said with a twinkle in his eyes which showed that he was joking. "I may even hear you preach some of these days." He turned and walked back through the swinging doors, leaving K.D. in the middle of the hospital waiting room.

When K.D. regained his composure, he asked the young girl if she knew the way to the Ericson farm. She drew him a map, marking north, south, east, and west and all the points of interest along the way—an old elm tree on this corner, a little rock rise off on your left, the dairy barn, Reinschmidt's house, and the Ericson's mailbox. Then as if it were her duty, she assured him that he couldn't miss it. In the inner part of his brain, he mocked her for not understanding the vast difference between his world and hers.

10

Dance of the Combines

To his amazement, Pastor K.D. Garrett of the First Baptist Church found the girl's directions clear and the landmarks helpful. To add further to his amazement, he managed the pickup along the country road, shifting down and dodging the grain trucks which came roaring by on regular intervals and at emergency speeds.

Sooner than he expected, he found the Ericson mailbox and turned in at the gate. But when he looked up to survey the farm, he wondered if he were in the right place. Combines, huge and awkward combines, were all over the field, moving about by jerks and spurts, gobbling up great gobs of grain with front end mouths of many moving parts and spitting straw out the back. K.D. counted the combines at work in that one field, one, two, three, four . . . eight . . . twelve, thirteen, fourteen. . . . There were fourteen combines in that one field. Although K.D. had no concept of how much 300 acres was, or of how much one of those machines could harvest in an hour, he could tell that those fourteen machines would eat that field quickly.

He didn't know how to interpret what he was seeing. He had just left Abe who was very concerned about days and days of harvest ahead, and now all these combines were cutting his field. What had happened that Abe didn't know about? Maybe his wife, Mary Ruth, hired all the farmers who had already finished. Abe mentioned that as one possibility.

The pastor drove to the house and walked up the steps. Through the open door, he could see a flurry of activity, women scurrying about as if they too were caught in the hurry of harvest. He rapped gently at the door. In the midst of all the din, someone heard him and a tall, pleasant lady stepped outside. "Oh," she exclaimed as she saw him, "I'll bet you're Pastor Garrett. I'm so glad you have come. We heard such nice things about your sermon yesterday. I'm Mary Ruth Ericson." And she looked deeply into K.D.'s eyes and smiled as if she had some kind of kinship with him.

After assuring her that he was Pastor Garrett, K.D. asked his first question. "Who are all those people cutting your wheat?"

"Neighbors," she said quietly continuing to smile. "Some from as far as fifteen miles away."

"So you have hired the people who have finished? Your husband said you might do that." K.D. wanted her to know that he had been to see Abe, and fulfilled his pastoral duties.

"Oh, no, they aren't finished. And we didn't hire them. They came over voluntarily to do this."

"You mean they left their own fields uncut to come over here?" K.D. was trying to understand.

"Yes," she said.

"But they wouldn't take time off to come to church yesterday," K.D. blurted out his feelings quicker and harsher than he meant to.

Mary Ruth smiled, and put her hand on his arm. "But church yesterday was not a life-and-death matter. This may be. Abe is sick and we don't know what's wrong with him. He will just worry himself sicker with uncut wheat in the field. Our neighbors know this, and that is why they have come today. They are helping Abe get well."

K.D. wondered why Abe hadn't mentioned it. "Is this something you expected?" he asked.

"No," she said, "you never expect it. Almost every time in situations like this, it happens, but you can never expect it. You must learn not to depend on anyone else; then you are even more grateful when you get unexpected help."

"How long will it take them to finish?" K.D. wanted to know.

"They'll finish today sometime," she said, "and then Abe can concentrate on getting well."

"Who are the women?" K.D. was still trying to understand what he had just heard.

"Wives. They all brought dishes and we are preparing dinner for the men now," she told him simply.

"Oh, the men will quit soon for the meal, then?" he asked.

She smiled as if she enjoyed telling him these things. "During harvest when the grain is dry, you never quit for anything. We take the food to the fields and they eat right there."

The pastor suddenly remembered his mission. He had come to help her spiritually, but he couldn't think of a Bible verse that would cheer her anymore than she was; and the look on her face seemed to say that she was caught up with her prayers. So instead, he volunteered, "Is there anything I can do?" He offered as the pastor, but he was also caught up in the mood of the morning. All that show of country charity had made him feel more charitable.

As she thought about his question, she understood his need to help. Finally, as her eyes wandered around the farm, she thought of something. "In all the excitement today, I completely forgot to milk the cow. Abe always does that, and I just forgot. She is standing out there by the barn now, probably suffering a bit from too much milk in her bag and wondering if everybody has gone crazy. Would you mind milking her for me? She doesn't give all that much, but she does need milking."

K.D. agreed quickly, partly because he didn't know what milking a cow entailed and partly because he was feeling almost indestructible at this moment with all the proficiency going on around him.

Too soon for him to stop to think about it, he had a bucket in his hand and was standing by the cow. After all, how difficult could this be? He knew where the milk came from and now he only needed to know how it came out. He did have a bit of a problem trying to decide which side of the cow to approach; but since both looked the same, he decided it didn't make that much difference. He took off his jacket, hung it in a safe place, and ran his fingers down the cow's side. He was surprised to find the feeling pleasant. He always thought cows would be rough and coarse, rather than soft and almost silky. He grabbed one of the teats and pulled as hard as he could, but nothing came out. The cow flinched ever so gently as if he were hurting her, so he stopped. He tried another but with the same result. The next time, he tried squeezing instead of pulling, but that was even less effective than pulling. He decided that he was doing something wrong. Maybe there was a hidden spigot. He started walking around the cow looking for it, when he saw Mary Ruth leaning on the fence, smiling.

"I'm sorry," she said, "but there is a trick to it. Let me help you." She slid through the gate, sat down on the left side of the cow, and started working at the teats. The milk came in steady, strong streams which rang against the sides and bottom of the bucket as they hit. Like a concert pianist, Mary Ruth played a tune with the streams of milk on the empty bucket.

K.D. stared in injured inquisitiveness. She explained her actions. "It's a combination movement. You pull and squeeze at the same time. It's hard to learn, and almost useless anymore. We are probably the only family in Wheatheart who still milk a cow by hand." But her explanation did not make him feel any better.

When she had finished, he carried the half-filled bucket back to the house for her. She introduced him to each of the ladies, who greeted him cheerfully, as if they had awaited his arrival in Wheatheart; but after the greeting, each in turn went back to scurrying about the meal preparation.

K.D. could sense that he was in the way, so he stepped back outside with Mary Ruth, stood by the door, and invited her to join him in prayer. Silently but eagerly, she bowed there in the sweet odor of the bermuda grass lawn. The pastor's prayer was filled more with thanks than requests, and he suddenly remembered that he had not thanked God for anything for the past week.

As he started to walk away, Mary Ruth called to him. "Pastor, would you like to stop by and tell Abe that the neighbors are cutting our wheat today?"

At first, he appreciated the request. Now she needed him for something he could do. He could be of help, save her some time; but as he looked at her, he knew that wasn't the case. She had time to tell Abe herself, and she *wanted* to tell him. It would be a thrill for her to see Abe's face when he heard this piece of information, to know what his neighbors thought of him. But Mary Ruth had asked K.D. to share the moment instead. At first, he wanted to protest. He wouldn't deny her the experience. But as he looked at her again, something welled up in his mouth so he couldn't form the words of protest. He said only, "Thanks."

Driving out toward the gate, he stopped in the lane, turned the engine off and watched the harvest longer than he ever thought he would. There was really something beautiful about all the activity; the combines were more graceful than he had originally thought. The contrast of the red and green machines, against the gold of the grain and blue of the sky, painted a fascinating picture. But it was more than a flat work of art. There was movement too. Although these operators had never all worked in the same field before today, they each knew what the other was doing, so that the operation looked as if it had been choreographed by a master. After several minutes of watching, K.D. labeled it the "Dance of the Combines," and drove back to the hospital to tell Abe the good news.

Abe responded the way K.D. thought and hoped he would. For a moment, he was too taken back to respond, and then he relaxed more than K.D. had seen him do, except when he had read the familiar Scripture earlier in the day.

Although K.D. enjoyed the moment, he felt uncomfortable being there. He saw there was more significance in this for Abe than he had expected there to be, and he felt almost as if it was too sacred to be shared. Finally, in awkwardness, the pastor said, "The neighbors gave you a lot today."

Abe sighed and said very quietly, as if only for himself, "I gave them a lot last fall."

Then K.D. knew he shouldn't be there, so he left without even saying good-bye.

11

The Dew Drop Inn Cafe

The next morning, K.D. Garrett awoke because he was the pastor of the First Baptist Church. He had duties to attend to. He had sick parishioners and others to care for. He dressed quickly but still taking the necessary time to tie and retie his tie until he got it exactly right.

He marched up the stairs and out the door into the early morning sunlight, the ever present and almost acceptable elevator din and the never acceptable smell of freshly cut wheat. He climbed into the old white Chevy pickup with only one swat at cleaning a spot to sit, drove down Main Street, parked right in front of the Dew Drop Inn Cafe, and marched in to have his breakfast.

Because he was earlier than usual, he saw some faces he had not seen before; he saw too the urgency in eating, the abrupt manners and the conversation. Regardless of the crowd, the conversation was always the same. Delivered in nasal twang, covering subjects foreign to K.D., and spoken always with just a hint of cynicism, the conversation was always the same. Although he was almost an hour earlier than he had been before, Rosemary, the waitress, was just as haggard, curt, and noncommunicative.

For K.D. there was a difference today, because he was different and also because Scott Garland was there. When K.D. walked in, Scott invited him over to sit with him and two other men at a corner booth. There were no introductions, but that really didn't matter much. The other two men were obviously busy with talk of harvest. They were dressed in greasy jeans hooked just beneath their over-sized stomachs, old ragged dress shirts with the sleeves rolled up just past the bulging biceps, and seed company caps. Scott Garland had a relationship with those two men and he had a relationship with K.D. But since the two men and K.D. had no relationship with each other, there was no need for introductions.

Scott was friendly and refreshing. He asked questions and listened as if the answers meant something. Although he spent most of his concentration eating a little faster than usual, as he explained to K.D., he still took time out to look up and smile in the appropriate places.

At first, he asked K.D. the mundane questions. "How do you like Wheatheart?" "How is the old pickup doing?" and "How many did you have in church Sunday?" For most of the questions, K.D. was politely dishonest, trying to say what he thought anyone would want to hear about his hometown. But on the final question, he chose to answer with the truth, but he also chose to document it with a hint of humor. Unfortunately, when he tried that combination, his voice rose higher than he would have liked, and he spoke with more volume than usual. Unfortunately too, he chose to speak the truth at the rare moment when all the conversationalists stopped at the same time to draw a breath. Into that momentary hush, K.D. blurted, "Eleven women, one man, and four children."

Everyone there broke out in laughter. Perhaps some understood the context, but for those who didn't, it was still funny.

K.D. tried to hide his embarrassment, but he was too close to anger to be able to conceal much. Scott laughed too, but he sensed K.D.'s emotion and reached over and grabbed his arm as if to say, "At least, I am laughing with you."

After the laughter died down, Scott said to K.D. "Tell me about your seminary education," and went back to his eating.

For more than a week which seemed more like than a year, K.D. had had the opportunity to think about life back in the seminary but not talk about it, because no one had asked. Now, with the pleasant and interested Scott Garland at his side, he could think about the seminary, because someone else wanted to know.

He spoke of his classes and his professors and his goals and dreams. He even put some of the recitation in the familiar language of abbrevations known only by those in the know. He spoke of Psych and Soc and Theo classes, realizing that those were not universal terms, but appreciating the opportunity to be specific.

As he spoke of those things, the harvesters across from him spoke of acres and bushels and breakdowns and old Johnnys and new Masseys. Scott Garland listened to both conversations, sometimes one at a time and sometimes both together. Although both parties vied for his attention, he held them equal as if he were a moderator in an important debate.

Just as K.D.'s breakfast came, Scott excused himself and went off to his business, leaving K.D. contented with his pleasant memories, yet stranded at a table of harvesters who still talked of bushels and acres.

K.D. managed the situation by ignoring the reality and the present as much as he could. He divided his time between remembering how pleasant seminary life was and thinking how kind Scott Garland had been to remind him. "He will be my friend here," K.D. told himself when his ear accidentally tuned into the general conversation going a new but familiar direction.

"When are you fixing to finish?" someone was asking.

"Thursday now, if we have good luck," one man answered. "We sent both combines down to Abe's yesterday and lost almost a whole day."

"Me too," a few others volunteered.

K.D.'s mood changed and he almost felt ashamed of himself. He didn't need to shut these men out. These were the men who had taken their precious time to do something noble, and that kind of nobility unites people. "These are friends, not enemies," K.D. thought. "I must learn that."

"How is old Abe?" someone asked.

"Pretty bad shape, I heard," another responded, making the whole thing sound worse than it really was.

"Is he going to make it?"

"Still touch and go," came the report.

K.D. was shocked and perhaps even amused by the answer. The man was giving completely false information. He obviously did not even know, but somehow felt it his duty to make a report, so he gave the worst one he could. K.D. wanted to correct the information, to tell them what Dr. Heimer had said, to tell them that he knew more about it than they did. But he didn't know them well enough to interfere, so he continued to eat quietly.

"That's too bad," they all agreed.

The next question was still about Abe, but sent the conversation a different direction. "How'd his wheat do?"

"Pretty good," was the general answer, and K.D. was pricked inside with just a bristle of pride that he knew the Ericsons. He was the pastor of the First Baptist Church and they were in his congregation.

"Well, maybe he's got the trick," someone said, and a ripple of snickers broke out in several pockets of the harvesters all around the Dew Drop Inn Cafe.

"Yeah," another said, on the verge of laughter. "Maybe we all ought to pull a tandem disc in front of our wheat drills every fall, rain or shine, like old Abe does." The snicker turned to laughter.

K.D. burned inside. For one thing, he did not understand the humor because he didn't know what was so unusual about Abe's farming methods. But even if they were different, he didn't understand the ridicule. These people had shown so much concern, some even making a sacrifice to help harvest his crop, and in an instant it all turned to ridicule.

"What kind of men are these?" K.D. wondered, as he paid his bill and walked out of the cafe as quickly as he could.

12

One More Contradiction

As he stood there and looked up and down Main Street as far as he could see in both directions, all the way up to the high school on the north, and south to where Main Street turned into just another country dirt road, K.D. Garrett was more confused than he had ever been in life. He could handle paradoxes; sometimes in the life of a thinking Christian, these are inevitable. But he couldn't understand contradictions. Although Main Street was empty of people and almost empty of pickup trucks, off in the distance the constant din from the elevators, with machinery groaning and engines roaring and people hollering, reminded him that hurry and urgency, the kind that breed selfishness, were just around the corner.

One day, in an act of simple charity, somebody breaks the selfishness and does something noble. But the next day he scorns it by scorning the one he served.

K.D. started to climb back into the white Chevy pickup but couldn't. Parked there in front of the Dew Drop Inn Cafe, it became a symbol of the whole town. It was modern transportation all right, capable of getting you to where you want to go as well as any automobile could, but it was crude. It was that crudeness disguised as sophistication that K.D. couldn't stand just then, so he slammed the door and walked off.

For more than two hours, he walked up and down the streets of Wheatheart, seeing everywhere contradictions he couldn't explain. Small crowded houses sat next to large brick or stone homes which looked out of place in their surroundings. In the backyards, the gardens grew lush with vegetables and flowers. But in the front yards, the bermuda grass lawns were almost bare from thirst—except in front of the big houses, where the grass, watered and tailored, provided a carpet which served the same purpose as a moat around a medieval castle.

Walking at random, his footsteps finally brought him to the post office; and although he checked the church's box, he did not feel much like the pastor. But as he pulled the mail out of the box, and sorted past the usual stuff—a package from the denominational headquarters in Oklahoma City, a catalogue from a church furniture store, and a letter from Brother Bob addressed to the congregation—he came to a source of joy. A letter addressed to the The Reverend K.D. Garrett, Pastor, First Baptist Church, Wheatheart, Oklahoma, carried no return address and no sender identification except for Rebecca's initials on the back flap.

Grasping the letter like a man in exile, K.D. studied the envelope, not anticipating what was inside—the letter was too precious for that. But instead, he was anticipating how he would feel when he discovered what was inside.

Still living in a land of his thoughts and expectations, K.D. remembered the reality of the post office when he felt a hand grasp his shoulder. At first he wanted to jerk away, but the grasp was more the kind you welcome rather than the kind you jerk away from, so he turned and looked into the burrowing eyes of Coach Rose.

Without any kind of greeting, Coach said gently and sincerely, "I want to thank you for all you are doing for the Ericsons."

This time, K.D. sensed more of a paradox than a contradiction. "How do you know what I have done?" he asked.

"I've been over to see Abe a couple of times, and I checked on

Mary Ruth." Coach said it as if he wasn't expecting any rewards. That's what he said with his mouth. But with his eyes he said to K.D., "You can talk about it if you want to."

So K.D. did. "Well, I'm not sure I did either of them much good." He wanted to sound just modest, but he was almost too sincere to seem so.

"Oh, you did a lot of good." Coach was assessing more than praising.

"I don't know. I don't know enough about hearts or Wheatheart to help Abe very much, and I can't milk a cow so I couldn't help Mary Ruth either." He wished he hadn't said that.

Coach didn't quite smile, but he almost did as he said, "I'll forget you said that if you want me to." Then he went on, "I've found in my business that being is more important than doing. That's how you're helping the Ericsons right now, and I thank you. I'm glad you're here."

With that, he started to walk out, but K.D. interrupted him with one further question. "How do you know the Ericsons so well?"

Coach turned back around, furrowed the brows around his burrowing eyes, tried to cover a tear growing in one corner, and answered, "We've suffered together." Then he went away.

K.D. studied yet another contradiction—the contradiction between the man he had just met and those in the cafe, but only momentarily, because he had to get to the letter.

Although the street was mostly quiet, he couldn't risk the possibility of an interruption, so he retreated to the pickup, drove up to the Methodist Church, parked in the shade of one of the cedars, and read his letter.

It was almost cool there in the shade, and the letter made him forget the heat. He took his time, reading and rereading, putting a different hue of meaning on each word and sentence with each rereading. Sometimes he read about a positive girl, self-sufficient and comfortable with her summer; but other times, he read about a girl who missed him as much as he missed her. Then he got angry with himself because he couldn't tell which reading was right, and he almost wished he hadn't gotten the letter at all.

The first part of the letter, several pages in fact, was a simple chronicle of Rebecca's activities since K.D. had left her for what she called the "Pollyanna world of a rural pastorate." Although K.D. tried to read too many meanings into each account, he still realized that she had written the details as a way of bringing her close to him, and he enjoyed the proximity to her life.

But near the end of the letter, she took a different tone as she turned to the present and future and became the young pastor's minister.

K.D.,

I am truly sorry to hear that Wheatheart is such a painful experience for you. I hate to see you in pain; but perhaps some pain is necessary.

When I was in high school, I ran track. The old coach, typical of the traditional image, was fond of yelling, "No pain, no gain." I never really understood nor believed him until recently.

Maybe in this process of growing up, we have to go through some pain. During my freshman year in college, I went home for the Thanksgiving break for a much-needed refresher; but instead, I discovered that I no longer had a toothbrush hanging in my mother's bathroom. She had thrown it away.

I shall never forget how I felt about that one small incident which only reminded me that I didn't really live there anymore. I was crushed and almost depressed for days. When I was a child, I always wanted to be independent; but when I had independence shoved at me, I longed to be a child again. I think the attractiveness of childhood and youth is that someone else sets the direction for us. In adulthood, we have to establish our own objectives. That is a scary thought, isn't it?

From your letters, I gather that at least part of the pain of the Wheatheart experience is that you have lost the comfort of the past, of being familiar and competent. Now, you have to discover new methods of dealing with people and situations, and that is always tough. Perhaps it isn't Wheatheart that you are struggling against, but making adjustments. But within ourselves and within the Scriptures, we have the power to grow. I shall pray for you because I care.

Rebecca

P.S. If Mrs. Strommer starts to flirt with you, just tell her that you're my fellow. R.C.

K.D. liked the letter until he got to the last section and that didn't make any sense. He read it over more often than he read the rest, but he still didn't know what she had said to him. Nevertheless, he put the letter in his pocket and the words in his heart and kept them there throughout the week as he went through the mechanics of being a pastor.

He visited Abe every day, lengthening his stay as he saw Abe's health improving. Although the two didn't have all that much to say to each other, they found a common ground in Scripture. K.D. loved the Bible and Abe knew he should, so K.D. spent his hospital visiting time reading Scripture to Abe, usually without comment or commentary.

The pastor also visited Mary Ruth on the farm every day. Although he enjoyed the visits, he felt awkward while he was there. She was so gracious to him that he always wondered if he was somehow behind in the game of giving. She showed him the farm, but in a gentle and accepting way. She explained that chickens lay only one egg a day and that fifty bushels of wheat an acre is a good crop, but that fifty-five is better, and that milk cows go dry of their milk a couple of months before a calf is born.

She fed him more than he really wanted to eat and kept his glass full of the iced tea she had brewed in the large-mouthed jars sitting in the sun. With each glassful, he went deeper into her debt.

There was one other problem with the Ericsons. Abe still wasn't satisfied even though his wheat was out. Now he was worrying about getting his ground plowed. K.D. couldn't understand the concern at all. All over town, the harvest was the urgency, but now it seemed that Abe was almost as anxious about plowing.

Regardless of whether the pastor understood it or not, he knew the anxiety wasn't good for Abe, so he made another visit to Dr. Heimer. This time they met in the hall of the hospital. Embarrassed a bit by the situation, and in consideration of the sick, K.D. talked quietly, until Doc told him to speak up so he could hear. Soon, talking louder than he would have chosen to, K.D. told the doctor of Abe's anxiety. Doc Heimer laughed a bit, and quit being a doctor and started being a teacher. "Now, Preacher," he said, sounding almost like some of the harvesters down at the Dew Drop Inn, "you're going to learn to understand these people. Abe, there, doesn't have a bit of blood. He has red dirt in those veins, filtered through his skin. He has farmed it, and dug in it, and lived it, and eaten it all his life, and now it's more than what he does, it's what he is.

"Frankly, I don't understand it either. I just don't know why someone wants to love dirt as much as these farmers do, but they do. They want to be the best farmers. At times, you may think they are in competition with each other, but they aren't really. They just like to see that dirt farmed up nice. It is kind of like me seeing a good-looking set of stitches or you hearing yourself preach a good sermon. Sure, he's anxious and he will be till the day he dies. And there is nothing you or I can do about it. He'll get his ground plowed. They always do, but then he will find something else to worry about." With that, the doctor walked on down the hall, looking for someplace to spit, and K.D. went home to ponder one more contradiction.

Between hospital visits and his visits to the farm, K.D. still found time to prepare a sermon. After last Sunday, he didn't give the sermon preparation top billing, but he didn't cheat it either. He chose the topic on Tuesday, during one of his readings with Abe, "The Inerrancy of Scripture," and he did his research thoroughly, both in the Bible and in supplementary texts. He stayed at church one night and prepared a fine outline. In fact, he prepared seven pages of outline—solid material with quotations and references which proved beyond any doubt that every jot and tittle came from God.

But this week, he didn't spend all the extra time on delivery. He had prepared the sermon. He had the notes, but he simply was not going to build his expectations too high by overdoing the preparation. If necessary, he could read to those eleven women, one man and four children.

With that thought, he climbed up into his bed rather early Saturday night and fought himself into a troubled sleep sometime after three o'clock.

13

Seven Pages of Notes

On Sunday morning, Pastor K.D. Garrett of the First Baptist Church awoke to the ringing of church bells, and for a moment couldn't locate himself in his early morning surroundings. He remembered that he was in Wheatheart, but he couldn't remember bells on top of the church. But then he realized that the sound was coming from further down the street, from the Methodist Church, and since they started earlier than the Baptists, he even had another few minutes to sleep.

Later, when he walked outside, he realized why he had heard the church bells; during the night, the elevator din had stopped.

For the second week in a row, he beat the Sunday School crowd to the church, but again decided to spend his time in the study in the adjoining building rather than mingling. Even though he was going to be disappointed, he still wanted to wait as long he could.

He tried going back over his seven pages of notes, but somewhere in the middle, when he stopped to look up a Bible reference, his mind took off a new turn, the authorship of the Book of Hebrews, and he spent most of the hour pursuing that instead of his thoughts for the day. It didn't matter; he still had the notes. So when he heard the piano signaling the time to enter, he tucked his Bible under his arm and walked through the passageway and into the sanctuary, looking for the empty pews.

But he couldn't find them. All over the auditorium the pews were packed , and as the pastor walked up on the podium to take his seat in the cushioned chair beneath the baptistry painting, he heard Jeff Devine announce, "We have 213 people present. Largest crowd since Easter. Praise God! Now let's all show the new preacher how we can sing."

The new pastor sang too, but in a daze. His eyes were bleary, from tears of joy or fear, he couldn't tell which, and he had trouble distinguishing people. Other than Mary Ruth and Mrs. Strommer, and a few people he had met last week, everyone else ran together. He knew he had seen some of them, in the Dew Drop Inn Cafe, in the stores during his first day visit, and at Mary Ruth's harvest dinner, but he couldn't remember any of them in context.

Although he was more concerned about himself than anything else, he could still tell that the singing was lively and loud. People sang as if they weren't afraid of who was listening. With precision, the ushers took the offering. One of the deacons offered the sched-uled prayer, including such items as the harvest, Abe Ericson's health, and forgiveness from sin. And as the deacon brought the prayer to a close, the new pastor added one more note of thanksgiv-ing under his breath, "Thank God for sermon notes."

With that, K.D. Garrett, Pastor of the First Baptist Church and formerly of the Fort Worth Seminary, stepped to the pulpit and greeted the people. With confidence warranted by preparation, he read a brief text, and looked down at the first point of his seven pages of notes. At that exact moment, one of the ushers flipped a switch on the back wall and sent electricity to the big squirrel-cage fan behind the pulpit. The fan sent a burst of cool air throughout the auditorium and a gust of wind toward the pulpit. Seven pages of carefully worked, carefully documented notes went flying about the room.

K.D. Garrett, scholar of God, wanted to cry; but the new pastor, continuing to look calm, burst into sermon and eleven minutes later pronounced the final "Amen" of the benediction.

As he greeted his congregation at the door, everyone was friendly. If he had had his wish, K.D. would have rushed, but the people were in no hurry. They all wanted to greet him and say kind things to him. They wanted him to know them by face and name. And they wanted to talk to each other.

Harvest was over. Almost as suddenly as it had begun, it ended. The completion of harvest always brings relief. Some years it brings happiness, and this was such a year. People stood around in the church and out on the yard and talked of bushels and acres, and they weren't in a hurry.

Almost everyone told K.D. that they had enjoyed the service, but they smiled when they said, "Nice talk, young man." . . . "Bless you." . . . "Thank you." . . . "We enjoyed it." And Mrs. Strommer said, "Well, young man, you're going to have to learn to preach without those notes."

By one o'clock after more than an hour of hanging around the church, everyone had gone off to his special afternoon. K.D., who had turned down seven invitations to Sunday dinner, went back into the sanctuary, gathered his scattered pages of notes from the pews and floor, walked home, lay on his bed staring up for a long time, and then spent the rest of the afternoon reading, writing a letter, and rereading one.

14

Sunday Dinner

Mary Ruth had dinner at the hospital with Abe. In Wheatheart, the hospital food was as good as you could get in the cafe. Doc Heimer's orders. "Just because a man is sick, he doesn't have to be miserable," the doctor said. And so the hospital hired Mrs. Rheinhart, one of the best cooks in town, to run the kitchen.

Mary Ruth filled Abe in on the church service, beginning with the prayer for his health and ending with the eleven-minute sermon. Then almost as an afterthought, she mentioned the notes flying about the church. As soon as he heard it, Abe laughed. Mary Ruth decided to laugh too, and soon they were laughing together. It was good laughter, the relaxing kind that makes you feel better even when you're sick. As they began to calm themselves, Mary Ruth wanted to make sure that they weren't just laughing at the new pastor, so she said, "But honestly, didn't we make a lot of mistakes when we were just starting something new? What about you when you started farming? Didn't you do dumb things at times?"

Abe thought about it for a while and said, without bragging, "No, not really. Most of us started in farming so young that we just grew up with it. It's different to make those kinds of mistakes when you are six."

But Mary Ruth wouldn't let it drop. "Yes, but there was something." She said it like she was teasing him.

After a while, Abe did think of something; at first he didn't want to say it, but then he did. He just blurted it out, "When I was a new father."

Mary Ruth only smiled, but Abe knew he should go on. "To tell you the truth, when we brought him home, I was scared to death. I'll bet I held him like he was a sack of chicken feed. Maybe I was a little awkward as a father." He said that like he wanted her to argue with it.

She did. "Yes, Abe, but being a father isn't so much what you do, but how you feel, as long as they know how you feel; and Jimmy Charles knew how you felt." She stopped for a moment and listened to what she had said. Although she had spoken that name to herself every day for the past nine months, as far as she could remember, that was the first time she had ever spoken it to Abe.

He noticed that too, and after some silence, they both began to talk. Oh, they had talked in the months since Jimmy Charles had been killed in that football game in November. They had talked about wheat prices and the need for rain and calf feed and the progress of the plowing. But they had never talked about Jimmy Charles to each other or to anyone else. But now they filled the whole afternoon with talk, memories, plans, and feelings. They never cried, either of them, but they talked.

Each told the other of private inner thoughts—of the times they remembered Jimmy Charles, of expecting Jimmy Charles to walk in, of planning conversations with Jimmy Charles that would never take place.

All through the afternoon they talked, and if Doc Heimer had been there with his instruments, he might have noticed that Abe's blood pressure was lower and his heart was beating with an easier rhythm.

Once in the conversation, when both paused for more memory, Abe said simply to his wife, "Does he remind you of Jimmy

Charles?" He didn't have to say more. They were husband and wife.

After several seconds, she said, "Yes, but not really. But he's alive and he needs our love now." Then they talked some more of their memories and plans.

* * * * *

Mrs. Scott Garland went home after church to an empty house. Her husband was away for the weekend on a business trip. He had gone to Wichita to sell tractors, some big business meeting that she wouldn't understand. He did call her last night and said he missed her, but he still wasn't home. Her son Michael was gone too, off to Oklahoma City for a weekend of fun and frolic. She didn't like for him to go, not when he was just completing high school, but she didn't have that much control when Scott was gone so much; and so she let him go rather than fight.

Once alone in the empty house, she undressed, hung her nice clothes up very carefully, and put on an old pair of shorts and one of Scott's shirts.

She checked the refrigerator for her Sunday feast, first thinking she would celebrate and treat herself to yogurt. Although it wasn't expensive, yogurt was special because the Red Bud didn't stock it, and she had to go into Alva to buy a large quantity.

But instead of yogurt, she reminded herself just in time of some homemade cottage cheese Mrs. Reinschmidt had given to Scott in appreciation for one of his civic activities. It was good. The curds were larger than the commercial kind, and it had a mild tartness which made it unique. "It ought to be good," Mrs. Reinschmidt had said. "It hung on my clothesline in the Oklahoma sunshine for two days."

After she finished her feast, Mrs. Garland went out back to the pool, the only private pool in all of Wheatheart, stretched out on the deck and wondered what it would be like to have Sunday dinner with a family in one of the small houses up and down the block, with kids running about and a husband and wife teasing each other and being together.

Then she thought about church, and about the notes flying

about; and when she thought about K.D. going on with his sermon anyway, she liked him. That required courage and she admired him for that. It would have been easy to run away, to quit; but he didn't do that. He called up what reserve he had and did his best.

Then she thought about herself. Unlike K.D., she had been trying to ignore her problems and the source of her pain. She had somehow hoped the situation would correct itself without confrontation, but now she knew that would never happen. For there to be any chance that her husband would ever love her and only her again, she had to confront the problem herself. Nobody was going to do it for her.

Of course, if she confronted him, she ran the risk of driving him away completely; but all actions have risks. K.D. could have quit when the notes blew away, but he didn't. He ran the risk of failure. Although the sermon itself was not one of those you remember ten or fifteen years later, his going on made the service memorable and an inspiration.

As the summer sun moved across the sky and the afternoon grew warmer, she moved into the shade of an umbrella and planned her action. Since the young pastor had become her model, she would begin by going to see him.

* * * * *

Out at the Bradys' on the west edge of town, Charlie's wife, Hester, had killed two of the young roosters for Sunday dinner. They had invited their two sons and families over to celebrate the end of harvest and being Bradys. The fried chicken was good— tender, crisp, tasty, and it reminded Charlie of the old days. Almost everything reminded Charlie of the old days, but the chicken helped trigger both memory and imagination, turning "the old days" into "the good old days."

Since Charlie's mind was conditioned to remember stories, he could remember back almost to the time of his birth in 1915. The conversation around the table would have flowed without Charlie's memories, but the stories helped it along and turned a Sunday dinner into a two-hour ceremony. Of course, everyone there had

SUMMERWINDS

heard at least one version of all of Charlie's stories before, but they
listened again because they were his children and because harvest
had ended.

When even the scratchers and the necks of the two fryers had
disappeared from the plate, and the fresh dewberry cobbler was
being dipped, still warm from the pan, Charlie started a new story.
"Darndest thing happened in church today." And he started to
chuckle to himself. Hester, who had been there too, blushed ever so
gently at the reminder, but kept on dipping the cobbler for her
grandchildren.

As Charlie searched his mind for the right method for developing
this new story into his repertoire, wanting to get it right the first
time through—the right words, the right gestures, and the right
facial accent at the punchline—he suddenly remembered K.D. and
thought about how frustrated and embarrassed and maybe even
hurt the new pastor must be right now. After that thought he went
on, "Boy, those fresh dewberries take me back. Your mother and I
planted that patch out there in 1939. We kept trying to raise
something on that old sandy corner, but we were growing old and
not anything else. Blew all the time, and I hated to hoe. I always
sunk in almost to my boot tops. Well, we planted a few of those
dewberry vines and by the end of the summer they had covered the
whole sandhill. Best farming I ever did and I just stumbled into it."

Later in the day, when Charlie thought about what he had done,
he couldn't remember ever changing in the middle of a story, not
intentionally anyway. He might have changed once in a while when
he forgot somewhere in the middle which story he was telling, but
never on purpose. Not until today. But that young preacher was just
so sincere that Charlie couldn't add any more to his hurt. Then he
thought of the stories he had been telling for years and decided to
eliminate some which might hurt people. It didn't matter that
much; he had so many stories that it wouldn't bother him to drop a
few, and it wasn't right to take a chance of hurting someone else just
to tell a story.

* * * * *

Mrs. Strommer had dinner out on the farm with her daughter's family. They talked about the church service, but she didn't make a big deal of the note incident. She had told K.D. what she had to say, and there was no need going on about it.

Instead, she talked about how neat he kept his room, and how good-looking he was, glancing frequently toward her granddaughter, Carol Anne.

* * * * *

Around the dinner table at the Goforths' house, Delbert told the rest of the family about the church service because no one else had been there. They enjoyed the account of the blowing notes, partly because Mr. Goforth's harvest rush at the elevator was over, and partly because of the way Delbert Ray told the story. He didn't talk that much about the pastor's hurt look or even about the sermon, but about how the papers blew through the air, floating around and landing on people.

When the family had finished laughing, Mrs. Goforth said, "It sounds like church is going to be fun this summer. Maybe we ought to go next Sunday." And they started making plans. Delbert spent the rest of the week wondering why his dreams always seemed to come true lately.

* * * * *

Vince and Elizabeth Ann Benalli drove into Oklahoma City that Sunday afternoon after church. Although both of them could have been free from harvest responsibilities, they still participated in the festivities. Each summer Vince drove a grain truck for one of the local farmers. The farmers needed the help, and since he was the high school principal, he needed to know what the community held dear. Elizabeth Ann went back down to the Farmer's State Bank and worked two weeks as a teller. She could handle the position well, since she had been a teller herself, until she became the president nine years ago. Before her early retirement a year ago, she had hired the two regular tellers. Most of the year they were bank tellers, but during harvest, they were farmers' wives first, so Elizabeth Ann went back down to the bank to let them fulfill their roles

Now that harvest was over, the Benallis could afford the luxury of a leisurely few days in Oklahoma City. Mostly, they would lie around the hotel swimming pool and read and talk. But they would also see what live theater was available that time of year, and they would shop, not so much because they needed anything but because they wanted the feeling of owning something they had bought in Oklahoma City. In that desire, they were like the rest of the people in Wheatheart.

Enroute, they talked about the church service and the blowing notes. They talked about youth and school, past and present; and they talked about life with each other. Somewhere after they had passed through Kingfisher, Vince turned philosophical. "Ever since I started teaching, it always seems like I cultivate a very special relationship with a student every few years. I don't know what it is, but somehow the two of us just seem to hit it off, and I become more than a teacher. I become a role model. . . . I was thinking the other day that I really haven't had one of those special students for quite some time, except of course, for Jimmy Charles," and he hesitated, partly because he needed to. "But this young pastor seems like someone we could get close to," changing the pronoun and the tone ever so slightly.

Beth Ann noticed the change and agreed. They began to make plans about how they could get acquainted with K.D. Garrett, partly so that they could help him understand some things about Wheatheart that had taken them more than twenty years.

* * * * *

Throughout the rest of the afternoon, in all the houses in Wheatheart, the people talked, and slept, and read the paper, and watched the baseball game on T.V., and remembered the notes flying about.

All except for K.D. Garrett, who lay on his bed, hating Wheatheart for the way it made him feel.

15

Notes From a Deep Hole

In the basement room which served as the pastor's retreat, K.D. spent the afternoon interacting with the people in his books until he found enough inner peace to write to Rebecca.

As before, he wrote of the future when he would be a recognized scholar, poised, respected, admired.

From there he wrote of the week—of combines in the fields and breakfasts at the Dew Drop Inn. Although he did not pause long enough in his thoughts to judge the way he felt about those things, he did manage to keep the narrative light and even at times a bit humorous—until he came to the morning sermon.

There he paused, lay on his bed, stared at the ceiling for a long time, and finally wrote:

Notes From a Deep Hole

Words are deceptive. There is a vast and profound difference between humility and humiliation. Once, Dr. Criswell came to the seminary and I stood beside him, talked with him, and I was not afraid to be humble in the presence of one who had earned my respect.

Today, my sermon was wiped out by a seventeenth century cooling device. Just as I stood to convince people that God had written the Bible, some mere man, a man that you have never heard of, destroyed me with a simple flip of the switch.

My notes blew all around. I struggled on, not in humbleness but in humiliation. Why must I live in crudeness and be reduced to its level? Of what value is intelligence and thought and dignity?

Your letter to me is worn out by now. The ink is smeared on the pages, but the words are burned in my mind. Since I cannot see your eyes as you write, I am carried to extremes with every word and sentence, from distress to bliss; I cry and I laugh, and I enjoy it all.

Always before when people spoke harshly to me, I protected myself by building a personal fortress of self-justification and rationalization. Your words are the harshest I have ever experienced, because I can't build the fortress. For some reason, I have run out of stone and mortar, and I stand before your words naked and wounded and bewildered. Not bewildered because you said those things to me, but bewildered that I can't build the fortress anymore.

I miss you, because I miss who I am when I am with you.

Write again.

Love,

The Persecuted One.

16

The Summer Winds

The next morning, Pastor K.D. Garrett of the First Baptist Church was roused from sleep by a gentle but persistent rapping at his door. Charlie Brady had come to take the Rev. to breakfast.

K.D. dressed quickly, tied his tie only once and went. Charlie stepped through the door of the Dew Drop Inn first, stopped in the doorway and announced in a loud voice to the room full of men and Rosemary, "This is Rev. K.D. Garrett of the First Baptist Church. He's is a friend of mine and if anybody picks on him, I'll whip your butt."

The crowd hooted various derisions, and Charlie read them all as acceptance. He took K.D. around table by table introducing him to each man and telling enough of a personal story about the person that K.D. could at least remember the story, even if he couldn't remember the name or face. Then they sat and ate, and K.D. could not believe the change in tone from what he had felt every time he had been here before. And it was caused by something more than his being with Charlie. Where before there had been a sense of urgency, today there was a sense of leisure. These were the same people as before, but now harvest was over, and their world was on a different time schedule. Men had not come to eat but to talk, and they did. They still talked of bushels and acres, but they also talked of prices and government and high school football.

When they talked of the government, they spoke of men who either didn't care or weren't smart enough to discern. When they talked of football they talked of a genius, cold and calculating, stern and austere, a one-dimensional man without emotions or feelings, committed to victory and nothing else, and they worshipped him because of those traits.

When they talked about the government, they didn't name the men, but when they talked about football they did, Coach Rose; and K.D. was beset with yet another contradiction. In his two meetings with Coach, he had seen none of these traits; but these men knew him better, had played for him, had sons who had played for him, so surely they knew.

K.D. decided not to pursue the contradiction right then. Besides, he didn't have the time.

"Hey, Preacher," someone directed the conversation to K.D. "You're a smart man, educated and all. I've been wondering something. You preachers tell me that God created everybody?" Instructed by an instinctive crude skill of persuasion, the questioner stopped and waited until K.D. confirmed that first premise.

"Now, you preachers also tell me that God plans out all the rain and the weather?" Again, he waited for K.D.'s confirmation. Although K.D. was not completely satisfied with the simplicity, he still had to agree with its basic accuracy. The questioner went on.

"Well, I was thinking about all those starving people over in Africa. They say they are out of food. Well, if God would just let it rain here at Wheatheart, we could raise enough extra wheat to feed them all. Now that sounds to me like a good deal. I am not asking for the right rains everywhere, but just here in Wheatheart.

"I ask you, does it make sense that God would let all those people starve when our land sits out here capable of producing a whole lot more if we just had the moisture?" With that the speaker leaned back in his chair, pleased with himself.

K.D . could tell from the stares and the quietness in the room that the questioner was not the only one who wanted an answer. But how could he answer at this place and this time? How could he put together a two-minute sermon on general and special grace and the problem of sin and the message of redemption? But he had to say something; so on an impulse he answered jokingly, "That's exactly what I am going to preach about one of these Sundays, and I just don't want to give my sermon away here. Why don't you come?"

Charlie Brady laughed right away, and patted K.D. on the back in approval, and soon the others, following Charlie's lead, laughed until the whole room had erupted in laughter, stronger and louder than it would have been had it not been at the end of harvest. Nevertheless, Charlie, acting rather quickly, finished eating and ushered K.D. out of the cafe, because he knew that they had let the young preacher off easily this time. They could have asked about why God wills that young men, good young men, should be killed in football games.

K.D. and Charlie spent the rest of the morning and part of the afternoon on a walking tour of all the businesses in town, and this time it was different from K.D.'s first attempt. And again the difference was something more than Charlies's presence. The clerks and owners had time to stop and chat and swap stories with Charlie and laugh and welcome the new pastor to town. And at each stop K.D. grew closer to his guide.

Then the next day, the two spent their time touring the farms in the old white Chevy pickup. Although the activity was anything but calm as the farmers prepared for the weeks and weeks of plowing ahead, they still weren't as busy as they had been the two weeks before, so they took time to chat and welcome the new pastor. The wives had time to serve them sun-brewed tea. And at each stop, K.D. enjoyed his guide even more, although by now he was beginning to hear some stories for the third and fourth time.

For lunch, Charlie's wife, Hester, had prepared a picnic basket, so the two stopped off at Wagner's Pond for food, conversation, and rest. Although it was not Keystone Lake or even the Arkansas River of Tulsa, Wagner's Pond was still a welcome place in the middle of a hot June day. The pond was isolated from the rest of the world by a big empty pasture occupied by a cow or two. The small body of water was large enough to cool the south breeze blowing across, and the willow trees were tall enough to provide shade. Since the two men were not in a hurry and the spot was pleasant, they took time to relax. Just to check his youth, K.D. threw a rock as far as he could. Just to check his maturity, Charlie skipped a rock across the water nine times. And when K.D. found skill more exciting than distance, Charlie gave lessons. Not only did K.D. learn to skip, even getting five skips once, but he even learned how to throw a flat rock into the wind and have it curve back toward the right instead of following the natural pattern of moving left. "It's all in the winds," Charlie said, "the summer winds. If you are ever going to survive in this game, you have to know how the winds blow."

After they had finished playing and learning, the two friends sat back down on the edge of the water. K.D. asked, "Charlie, what's happiness?"

The town storyteller took time to test his words and then said, "Well, in my lifetime, I've had one good bird dog, one good saddle horse and one good woman, and I guess that's about all the happiness any human deserves or maybe can handle." And with that he spent the rest of the afternoon telling stories about that good bird dog and that good saddle horse, and K.D. tried to assess what he had said.

On Wednesday, Mrs. Craig, the church secretary, came back to work; the church returned to two services a week; and everybody declared the harvest season officially over. Since Mrs. Craig acted more comfortable with her position than K.D. was with his, he decided to leave her alone and let her do whatever it was she was supposed to do, which seemed to be talking on the phone a good deal.

The pastor also found time to visit Abe in the hospital, but he felt a little guilty about it. The week before, K.D. had visited Abe a lot, perhaps because he needed the visits more than Abe did; but now that that had changed, going to the hospital was more of a duty than a fulfillment.

Mrs. Garland called and asked the pastor if he had time for a visit. He suggested five o'clock; she suggested eight, and they agreed.

When she finally came, the sun was just starting to disappear behind the western horizon, and the pastor's study had dimmed to that stage of light when it was still too bright to turn on the lights and too dark to distinguish as clearly as one needed to.

As she walked in the door, K.D. was struck with her beauty. He had remembered her from Sunday, but somehow in the more urgent and distressing matters of the day, he had failed to notice that she was a beautiful woman, the kind of woman who cares about the way she looks without being ostentatious. As he saw her, K.D. reminded himself of why Scott was such a pleasant and happy man. He had reason to be. Since he was already thinking about that, K. D. used it for an opener. After the usual greetings, he said, "I just want you to know how much I think of your husband. Since I have been in Wheatheart, I have really come to appreciate all he does for this town, including his support of my ministry. What a fine man he is. The two of you must be quite happy with each other."

She smiled, graciously thanked him for his compliments, and asked if they could talk about Sunday School classrooms. She knew it was too early to make plans for the fall with Brother Bob gone for the summer, but she was anticipating a larger crowd when school started. That room she had been in was rather small and didn't allow her much space to arrange the chairs in a circle. She wanted to know what K.D. thought about placement of chairs, and she listened as he recited everything he had ever learned in pedagogy classes about room arrangement and eye contact, and even about inductive study. When he had finished his speech, she thanked him sincerely.

As she got up to leave, K.D. was pleased with his first, in-study, pastoral session. But as she reached the door and started to say one more good-bye, she turned back, moved quickly to the chair across from the desk, dragged it around beside him, sat down, and said, "My husband is having an affair." By then she was crying, and the young pastor sat with a blank stare on his face and an even greater blank where his mind used to be.

In his feeble attempt to recover from that sudden turn of events and thoughts, he said only ridiculous things. "With whom?" he asked as if it really made a difference.

"With everybody," she said. "With anybody. He just goes out of town—Wichita, Oklahoma City, Tulsa—he knows a lot of people in all those places." And she cried even more.

The pastor handed her a tissue from out of the box he had discovered on the file cabinet. She wiped her eyes, and he fidgeted with his chair, moving it away from her so that he could regain the security of his own personal body space.

Without looking up, she told him the whole story. The trips, the lies, the town image, and the hurt. And then she told him of her love, of her commitment, of her deep devotion to her husband. She did not want to retaliate or hurt anybody. She just wanted her husband back. It sounded like such a simple request, and the pastor offered her simple suggestions to pursue. But in all the simple talk, they both knew she was asking for a miracle.

Trying to think of another line of questioning, K.D. asked, "Is he a Christian himself?"

She answered, "No, he's a salesman. He always knows the right words."

On that final statement, K.D. finished the session with prayer, and then she walked out, leaving him stranded there in the middle of his now darkened study.

Although he could not get that visit out of his mind, he was still able to function as pastor the rest of the week. He followed Charlie around, listening to the stories; he visited the hospital, first to see Abe and then others who were sick. He ran into the Coach once at the post office; and by accident he had breakfast again with Scott Garland, salesman. Again, Scott asked all the right questions, and K.D. enjoyed answering them, but not as much as before. He wanted to stop right in the middle of the conversation and talk to Scott about his actions and the way he hurt people. He thought that's what a real pastor would do, get to the root of the situation. That was what he knew he had to do, but he didn't have the courage, not then. Besides he would rather talk about the safe world of seminary classes and theology books, so he did. And that is why he had trouble sleeping every night for the rest of the week.

Not knowing what to expect on Sunday, the young pastor prepared a very nice sermon on the authorship of the Book of Hebrews. This was theology at its best, researched, thought through, documented, sound. He wondered if the people knew how fortunate they were to hear such a message. As he thought about that, lying in bed trying to fight himself to sleep on Saturday night, he suddenly realized how Hebrews would provide a nice text for a whole series; so he committed himself and the First Baptist Church of Wheatheart, Oklahoma to a study of Hebrews for the rest of the summer.

Vaguely, he remembered that Dr. Mitchell, the homiletics professor, had once said that no man should preach on Hebrews or Isaiah until he was at least forty. But since K.D. could not recall the context of that statement, he decided it wasn't appropriate to him, and so he slept as soundly as a pastor can sleep on a Saturday night.

Sunday service itself went without blemish. The music was the reassuring three hymns and a special. The pastor kept his notes in his Bible. The people sat courteously through the announcement of the series, and they sat politely through the sermon. They all looked intently at the young pastor, although some might have seen and heard other things.

At the door after the service, he greeted them, all 217 of them, including the whole Goforth family, and he waited patiently while they completed their visiting, some staying more than an hour after the service had officially ended. This Sunday, he received five invitations for Sunday dinner, but declined each.

Although he had one more sermon to preach before his week was through, Pastor K.D. Garrett of the First Baptist Church went back to the cool and quiet of his basement room and spent most of his afternoon writing a letter.

Notes From a Trustee

That afternoon, he spent more time on the letter than with the people in the books. He started with a detailed chronicle of the week, which provided him the opportunity to pause and dwell on memories worth remembering and perhaps even storing. Through the afternoon, he leisurely wrote and remembered, finishing with a reference to the present.

Notes From a Trustee

At least I have endured, and my persecution has turned to an uncomfortable complacency. This week I met the natives and they seemed friendly enough, but I still had to take my trusty translator to open the doors and direct the discourse.

I don't know about bushels and acres and I think I shall never know. In fact, I choose not to know. I can still be their pastor without that. The sermon today was good, better than they knew, a fair treatment of the authorship of Hebrews. Scholarly, even if I have to say so myself. But the response is only pleasant, a dull pleasant bordering on apathy.

I cannot read the faces or the signs. We set some kind of attendance record today, but I suspect they came to see the circus instead of hear the sermon.

But at least, I am doing my best. That is all I have to offer them. Neither they nor God can expect more.

I miss you. I miss your presence and your smile. If you were here, we would go to the new Eden, a place called Wagner's Pond, and we would talk and plan as we watched the water ripple and the stones skip.

In His name,
K.D.

18

Just Let 'Em Blow

The next morning Pastor K.D. Garrett of the First Baptist Church was again roused earlier than intended by a gentle, steady rapping at the door. This time the early morning guest was Delbert Goforth.

During the night, Delbert had put together a plan for getting the Ericsons' ground plowed so that Abe could rest. Using the Ericsons' equipment and diesel fuel, volunteers could come out sometime during the day or night and donate whatever portion of time they could afford. This would permit even the townspeople who didn't own any equipment to be able to volunteer. Delbert's dad liked the idea and Delbert thought several high school students would like to work, maybe even through the night, because of Jimmy Charles. All the plan needed was an organizer and a leader. Naturally, Delbert thought of his pastor.

K.D. was cautiously enthusiastic. He liked the plan, but he needed specific instructions.

"Just go out and sign people up," Delbert said. "That's all you have to do." And then Delbert made his second suggestion. Since the project needed a leader, maybe K. D. could go out today and work the first shift. That way, the news would spread all over the community pretty quick, and everyone would want to volunteer. "Just trying to make your job easier for you," Delbert told him.

Usually K.D. was too smart to get hooked into something like this. He knew it would only go wrong, but there was something about Delbert's shy confidence and his nonassuming but in-charge manner that made K.D. consider it. During the consideration, he accidentally uttered the wrong protest, "I don't know the first thing about driving a tractor."

"I'll show you," Delbert said. And the idea took root. Before going out to the Ericsons', the two stopped for breakfast at the Dew Drop Inn. K.D. was impressed at the way his young host was received. Although he was six or seven years younger than K.D., Delbert still walked into the Dew Drop with a certain boldness about himself. He wasn't arrogant, and he was a bit shy, but yet, he acted as if he belonged. The early breakfast crowd responded to him the same way. They didn't really go out of their way to recognize him, but they gave him more attention than they gave to most people who wandered into the middle of the constant conversation. K.D. might have been the only one who noticed it—the whole thing was so casual that it would have taken a stranger to discern the difference. It was as if these grown men, some crude and crass, had more respect for this young high school graduate than they really wanted to.

Delbert treated the reception nonchalantly. He ate breakfast a little faster than a gobble and sat impatiently until K.D. was finished and ready to go off "to plow Mr. Ericson's land," as Delbert announced just before the two left. Because of the collective attitude toward Delbert, the idea seemed to make more sense than if someone else had offered it.

When K.D. and Delbert got out to the farm, Mary Ruth was waiting for them. She had heard about Delbert's plan—his mother had called—and she was thrilled that anyone would have thought that much of them to offer such assistance. Still, she was a bit embarrassed that the pastor was going to participate. She just wanted to make sure that he had joined the endeavor willingly. All three of them laughed about that.

Delbert assured her that she had nothing to worry about. He would take care of the pastor, and with that announcement, the two of them went out to the barn. Together, they rode the tractor to the field where Delbert spent an hour demonstrating the proper techniques of staying in the track, turning corners, adjusting the depth of the plow sweeps, and manipulating the huge tractor. Like a little boy, K.D. sat on the toolbox watching more behind than in front. But before K.D. had managed to handle his initial fright of just riding on the moving tractor, Delbert leaped off and left him stranded in the middle of a wheat field.

Doing what he had been told, K.D. managed to get the machinery started once more and proceeded around the huge field. As he gained more confidence and his heart slowed enough that he was not aware of the pounding any longer, he took time to survey the operation. The field was huge; but since he didn't know acres and bushels, he didn't know how large. From atop the tractor seat, he was able to see across the prairies of the Wheatheart greater area. He saw little patches of green, hay he guessed, and pastures with grazing cows. But mostly, he saw the remnant of wheat. Everywhere he turned, he saw miles and miles of wheat stalks standing erect with their tops cut off, looking like one giant blond kid with a burr haircut. In his survey, he turned around and looked behind him at his own plow, and was quickly lost in fascination. The plowsweeps, that's what Delbert called them, burrowed themselves several inches beneath the soil, ripping the land and wheat roots up to the surface. Each sweep made giant trenches as it pulled the red dirt up and out of its bed of complacency; in the trenches behind the sweeps, the new dirt pulled from beneath the surface scurried about the furrow fighting other pieces of dirt and wheat stalks for a place to lodge. To his amazement, the operation behind the sweeps became alive, and K.D. found himself cheering for a particular lump of dirt or a cluster of roots.

As K.D. plowed through the morning, he knew he wasn't as skillful as Delbert at manipulating the tractor. Where Delbert had made round corners, letting the tractor do most of the work, K.D. made square corners and worked too hard at it, because he could not discover the exact moment to make his turn. He also moved the tractor too wide at times and left blotches of wheat stubble still standing, looking lonely beside their fallen compatriots. But other than that, he managed, and morning went quickly. Sometime in the middle of the day, Mary Ruth came out to the field, bringing him a sandwich, some delicious German chocolate cake and a huge jar of iced tea.

As he ate his lunch in the shade of the pickup, they talked. She began by saying, "I want to thank you for being special to Abe and me," and then she talked about the farm and he talked about the seminary. He wanted to stop and ask her about her son. He wanted to talk about Jimmy Charles so much that he felt angry with himself for talking about seminary days, but he didn't have the courage to stop and ask. So he kept talking about such things as theology classes and professors; and when he had finished, he plowed on until Delbert came to relieve him just before sundown. At times that afternoon, K.D. found his mind wandering to other things and other times, including Rebecca; but mostly he was so fascinated with the moment, the scenery, and the progress of plowing, that he filled his time and his mind with just looking. It was almost as if he were on vacation, and he didn't want Delbert to come so soon—until he stepped off the tractor and discovered that he was tired. His shoulders and hands ached and his legs buckled beneath him. He went home, took a quick shower, and went to bed, never once waking up during the night to remember that Mr. Strommer had died in that very spot.

The next morning, feeling refreshed physically and emotionally, he walked into the Dew Drop Inn for breakfast, and the crowd there applauded him. Before noon, he had enlisted more than enough volunteers to plow the Ericsons' land.

With efficiency, he plunged through his other pastoral duties of the day, including the scheduling of another appointment with Mrs. Garland. He chatted with the people in the stores up and down

Main Street. He stopped into the John Deere place to have the oil changed in the white Chevy and he talked with Scott Garland about the thrill of plowing all day. He made his hospital rounds, feeling that he was bringing good cheer to all, and about eight o'clock, headed over to the church to keep his appointment.

Mrs. Strommer was watering her tomatoes and begrudging the necessity. "Crazy country. We just never get enough rain. Couple of times I felt like just moving to some jungle where all you have to deal with is too much rain instead of never enough. Well, I hear you did a good job out at Mary Ruth's yesterday. I'm sure Abe's feeling better about that. May go home soon, I understand." The pastor had not heard that and he had spoken to Abe only that day, but he still trusted Mrs. Strommer's sources enough to believe her account had some kind of reliability.

She went on. "I see you're going to church again tonight. You're going up to prepare the sermon, I suppose." She wasn't really prying, but almost. Then she added, "I hear you're seeing Scotty's wife some. You may want to do that in the day instead of this time of night. Look how dry that is. Just huge clods. Not enough moisture to sprout a pea. I declare, it gets worse every year." And she continued to talk as the young pastor burned inside.

As he walked the almost two blocks to the church, he tried to get her words out of his mind, but he couldn't. "Just an old woman," he thought, "just an old busybody. Counseling should be private . . . how could she know?" But he dismissed the words and the incident as just the work of gossips. He still had to be the pastor.

The session with Mrs. Garland went almost like the last week. She cried and told him of the hurt and the shame. But this time it was different. He had a plan of action. He and Scott were friends. At least Scott was friendly enough. K.D. would just somehow have to manage the courage to go see Scott and talk to him about spiritual matters. He did not have to talk about this situation—not at the beginning. He could talk about spiritual things. That might help.

She consented, but only reluctantly; she was still frightened that Scott might find out that she had talked to the pastor, and she didn't really want him to know. She had made a commitment to do what she had to do to save her marriage, but now that she had to carry out that commitment, she had begun to lose her courage.

K.D. did not fully understand the commitment nor could she have ever explained it to him, but he assured her that he could handle the whole thing skillfully. On this note, she left happier than when she had come.

The next morning K.D. was so confident of himself that somehow he knew that even the post office visit would be productive. It was. He didn't see Coach, but he had a letter from Rebecca.

Just as he was thinking of the ideal place to read the letter, Wagner's Pond maybe, a couple of younger farmers that he had met once at the Dew Drop walked in. One went over to the window to conduct business and the other ambled over to K.D. "Hey, Preacher," he began, "how are you and Scotty's old lady getting along, anyway. She looks pretty nice to me. What do you think? Hey, how do you get into this preaching business anyway? You guys have a good thing going for you." He laughed a vulgar laugh, and walked out to spit on the curb.

K.D. stood in the middle of the post office, stranded with emotions he had never felt before. It was more than hate and anger, and hurt and defensiveness. It was all of those emotions tumbling all over themselves that added together to create a feeling unlike any he had ever felt before. On his way out to the white Chevy, he touched the letter he had placed so gently in his shirt pocket, and somehow he felt too dirty to even think about a person as pure as Rebecca.

Fighting against an urge to violence and retaliation, he managed to drive carefully enough to find Wagner's Pond, and he sat in exactly the same place he sat last week. But this time it was hot. The shade was more barren than he had remembered it, only spots; and the winds blowing across the water picked up heat instead of coolness and burned his skin.

He tried to read Rebecca's letter, but even that could not bring peace or happiness; so he put it away for a more complete reading later. He tried to pray and the hot winds blew the words back into his face, so he just sat there and stared across the water, sweating and hating this place.

After a few hours of this, he drove back into town, collecting his composure, if not his thoughts, and found his way to Charlie Brady's house. Fortunately, Hester was gone. Charlie was sitting in the living room in front of a water-cooled fan. He had his boots off, but he was still wearing his Stetson hat.

After the usual greetings and one quick story from Charlie, K.D. got down to business. "What are the people saying, Charlie?"

Charlie started to evade the question by reporting all the nice and complimentary things he had heard, but something in K.D.'s voice reminded him that this was serious. He thought for a moment, took off his hat, wiped his forehead with a faded blue bandana, and said, "Well, there is some talk about you and Scotty's wife."

"Who's heard it?" K.D. knew that sounded harsh, but he didn't mind, not just then.

"Everybody," Charlie reported truthfully.

"Who believes it?" K.D. asked, after he had time to think about Charlie's answer.

"Those who want to." Charlie was just reporting again.

Suddenly, K.D. wasn't the pastor anymore, but a small boy visiting a kindly uncle. He buried his face in his hands and cried out. "What am I going to do? How am I going to handle this?"

Charlie wasn't comfortable with K.D.'s new attitude, but he wasn't frightened by it either, so he talked on, being Charlie. "What have you done?"

"Why nothing!" K.D. was more defensive than he needed to be.

"Okay, then, two of us know that. And we are the only ones who really count."

"What do you mean?" K.D. was wishing he hadn't involved Charlie. He was afraid he was just too shallow to help much.

"You haven't done anything wrong, so you are the same person on the inside. Now you go ahead and do what you have to do and don't let those outside winds blow you around like that. Did I ever tell you about my getting saved?" Charlie asked, and went on without waiting for an answer. "For a long time, I wasn't the nicest guy around here. I made a lot of moonshine whiskey. Kept my family alive through the depression selling the stuff to all the neighbors before we had a doctor. Everybody knew the devil was going to get me before it was all over. But he didn't. Christ got me instead, in 1969 it was. Now a lot of people don't really believe it— they still know me as the old moonshiner, but that don't hurt me none. I am who I am on the inside, so I just let 'em blow."

That wasn't enough for K.D., to ease the pain and give him direction for his ministry in weeks to come; but he knew it was the best he was going to get, so he thanked Charlie and went home.

In the middle of the night, as he lay awake staring at the dark, something was suddenly so clear that he knew it must have come from God. "Why I still have the pulpit," K.D. thought. "I still have the pulpit. I can use the pulpit to put those people in their place." That thought took him through the night and the rest of the week.

From a simple text about bearing false witness, he wrote his sermon out word for word. He used the strong language of Jesus, words like *Pharisees* and *Hypocrites,* and he illustrated with Judas. By pouring himself into the message, he avoided the community and let the week pass quickly. This was more than a sermon—it was a passion, and he was ready for it.

Saturday evening he went up to the study just to check one last time that he had the gestures and accents in the right places. He read those strong words, growing more intense with each phrase. When he put the sermon notes aside and rested his head on the desk top, he remembered Mrs. Garland sitting in that very room, and he remembered Abe and Mary Ruth, and Delbert's project of plowing their land, and K.D. Garrett, pastor of the First Baptist Church of Wheatheart, began to cry.

As he sat weeping the tears of frustration, the phone rang, jarring him back into composure. It was his mother with the weekly news, the inquiries about his health and the weather, and instructions for living a life of safety and soundness.

After the usual exchange, he gathered his courage and asked,

"Mother, when was the last time you ever saw me cry?"

Since she could not see his eyes or know his heart, she answered him as if it were just another question. "I don't know, Dear. I think it was on your twelfth birthday. I remember you crying during the party, but I can't remember the reason. Do you?"

"No." K.D. couldn't even remember crying much less the reason, so they continued the conversation on a brighter note.

When they had finished talking, K.D. went back to his desk and tore his sermon notes into shreds, threw them in the wastebasket, and opened his Bible to the first chapter of Hebrews. Picking only the phrase, "These last days," he worked through the night preparing a message about the theories of millenium and rapture.

The next morning he preached that message to the whole 221 people who had come out to church. His ideas were sound, his words were clear, and his gestures were timely but unfeeling. Afterward, he forced a smile and shook hands with everyone, declined four invitations to Sunday dinner and went home to read a letter and write one.

19

Notes From the Dungeon

The letter from Rebecca which had been stored in his pocket and his hopes since Tuesday, was filled with good news because K.D. wanted it filled with good news. Since he did not seek any hidden meanings, he reread it several times but interpreted it only once. Her descriptions of events were so vivid and clear that he sat with her and held her hand during church services. He walked with her in the parks and along the streets. He shared the meals with her and tasted the same food she ate. He sat beside her during private devotions and helped her read through difficult passages.

This time there were no harsh instructions, only the accounts of her life and summer.

As soon as he was able, he wrote.

Notes From the Dungeon

Dear Rebecca,

Your letter came on Tuesday, but for personal reasons, I simply could not read it fully until today. It was the lifeline to a drowning man. I have been through despair this past week beyond what I can bear. It is something so nonsensically painful that I can't tell you about it now. Someday I shall.

I first planned the perfect retaliation. I would use God's pulpit for my own private gain, but I realized just in time that I cannot use the sacred desk for that. Each Sunday, I become more convinced that I am not really sure what God's pulpit is to be used for, but I know it is not for the pastor's private words.

But in the midst of licking my wounds, I read your letter, and because of you, I can face this town now, and these people, and these contradictions. I doubt that I shall ever make significant inroads, but at least I can face my duties.

But the combination of the cause of my despair and your letter has brought me face to face with a stark truth. I am in love with you and shall be for the rest of our lives. Whatever course of action that demands, we will pursue later, but I needed to make that pledge to you. From now on you become my sanity in a world gone mad. I am awaiting your reply.

Love,

K.D.

20

To *Define* Success

The next morning, Pastor K.D. Garrett was up before the traffic came, but not by much and not willingly. The first visitor was Mrs. Strommer who came for a simple reason, to invite him to have supper with her Tuesday evening. She had noticed that he was losing weight, and she wanted to help keep his strength up. Eating cafe food all the time wasn't healthy.

But with that simple reason for coming, she turned the visit into a major project. She helped him dust places he might not have known about; she helped him straighten the pictures around, mostly old photographs of her great uncles and cousins; and she filled him in on town news. Abe was going home. The plowing was coming along out on the farm. The women in the church had already begun to make plans for the Women's Missionary Union meeting in a few weeks. The farmers sure needed rain. Old Mr. Hadley, who had lived in the nursing home down in Alva for a long time, was back in the Wheatheart hospital, nothing really the matter, but he had just worn out almost everything that was supposed to work. Scott Garland had gone away for the week to help plan some big John Deere meeting that would happen right here in Wheatheart in about a month. Good for this little town. People here deserved good things to happen to them, because that was the kind of people they were—just good people.

When the cleaning and her news report were finished, she left, and the second visitor came. It was Vince Benalli. Before then, the pastor had only exchanged greetings with Vince and Beth Ann, but he wanted to get to know them. After K.D. had seen him in the congregation two weeks ago, Vince had become K.D.'s audience. Because Vince responded, K.D. preached to him, and they both got more out of the service.

Vince came with an invitation too. He wanted K.D. to come with him and Beth Ann to Canton Lake to water ski all day. "Pastors ought to take a day off at least once a week," Vince said, and that was enough to persuade K.D.

The day at the lake was everything they hoped it would be. The huge lake provided a buffer against the hot winds, and the three of them spent the day in the comfort of the boat and the water, mixing exercise with conversation and laughter.

They talked about high school, the students, the trends, the courses, and the football team which had won the state championship six out of the last twelve years, and that meant they talked about Coach Rose. They talked about the bank where Beth Ann had been president, until one day a year ago when she decided to quit and spend more time with her husband. They talked about seminary and Rebecca. By the time they had finished talking about all the safe things, they thought they knew each other well enough to talk about how they felt, the things no one else knows. As they were just trolling in the boat slowly watching the water splash up against the sides, Vince asked, "K.D., what have you had the most trouble with in the small town?"

"Gossip," K.D. said, not really wanting to say any more but still hoping that Vince would ask again. Instead, both Vince and Beth Ann laughed. It was the kind of laughter that told K.D. they understood and wanted him to join them in laughter. He tried, but he couldn't quite make it.

"I heard those stories," Vince said, and K.D. was able to laugh.

"I was only trying to do the right thing," the young pastor added, although he didn't need to.

"We know," Beth Ann said.

"Well, what do I do about it?" K.D. asked because he respected both of them enough to listen to their opinion.

"You handled it exactly right," Vince assured him. "People will think what they want to think, regardless of the reality. You just can't argue with a good imagination."

"You sound experienced," K.D. suggested.

The Benallis laughed again. "I've just adopted a new motto," Vince said. "Don't reason with unreasonable people."

K.D. sat silently watching the small waves banging against the boat as if they were angry, and contemplated why it was so difficult to take simple and sound advice. When he spoke again, he was in another mood. "Vince, you are an educator. What you and I do is rather similar, when you think about it. How do you ever know when you are successful?"

The Benallis smiled at each other and took each other by the hand. It was a casual gesture, but K.D. could read meaning into it beyond what he had implied with the question. Vince answered, "I suppose we all struggle with that sometime in our lives. I spent a year with that very question, and I think I have it answered." He paused, until K.D. almost had to encourage him to go on.

"The only thing that really matters in this world is the relationship. We have to define success in terms of the relationship, not the product."

With that piece of information for K.D. to ponder, they loaded the boat and drove back into Wheatheart, taking time to stop on top of the hill half mile east of town to watch the sunset and the lengthening shadows move over Wheatheart. From that vantage point, K.D. saw things he had missed before. The two elevators, one on each end of town stood like massive silent sentries, reminders of the lifeblood of the entire settlement. The hill up Main Street to the high school was bigger than when K.D. looked at it from the churchyard. Although the yards were dry from lack of rain, the town was still greener with more varied colors of green than K.D. had ever realized before. And the football field, watered and trimmed, flanked by eight stately light poles, was a lush oasis guarding the town from the north.

When the sun had set and they had driven back into town, K.D. thanked them sincerely for the day, and they thanked him sincerely for coming to Wheatheart to be their pastor.

He went to bed that night, woke up the next morning, and went through the rest of the week, still living in a land of contradictions. On one side, he had people like the Ericsons and Benallis and Charlie Brady who obviously liked him and encouraged him. He could pastor a church full of people like that. Sometimes he did not understand their ways or even their advice. He would never be completely one with the Ericsons simply because he would never know about acres and bushels, no matter how hard they tried to teach him. He wasn't sure he understood Charlie Brady's compulsion to tell stories, most of them over and over again. And he definitely didn't understand what Vince Benalli had meant when he said the relationship is the main thing that matters. But he did notice that Vince was one of the most relaxed men he had ever met. And that in itself was a contradiction. School principals shouldn't be that relaxed. What had he learned that was worth knowing?

On the other side of the ledger, he had to deal with the crude— the vulgar laughter in the post office, the Dew Drop Inn breakfast talk, the crumbling awnings and unpainted buildings along Main Street, and the constant talk of farms and football. He could never be the pastor of the crude. To them he was a nuisance, earning his place by being the object of their ridicule and off-color humor.

With the first group, he felt he had no ministry because they didn't need him. They had greater control of the situation than he did. To the other group, he had no ministry because they would never allow him into their closed world. They used their crude humor as a shield from anything dignified or holy.

Then there was Mrs. Garland. He hadn't really thought of her since that day in the post office, but only of himself and the damage done to his reputation as a young minister. Surely, she knew of the gossip; this was her town and she would have heard it before he had. He wondered what had gone on inside her house, inside her soul.

He really wanted to help her, but how could he? She had her problems before he had come to Wheatheart, and she would probably have them long after he was gone.

What help could he be to such people?

In less than a month, he would be pardoned from this incarceration and he would go back to his life of scholarship, preparing himself for the real ministry ahead.

But these people would go on with their lives, with all their problems and strange ways.

It was with this thought that he went around the corner of the house to have supper with Mrs. Strommer on Tuesday evening. When he got there, he was surprised to discover that he had been set up. They weren't alone. Her granddaughter, Carol Anne Bray, just happened to be in town for the evening and just happened to be there for supper too. In fact, Carol Ann had prepared most of the meal. She was talented that way. Good cook, good singer, good pianist, good student. She had already had her teeth straightened, and was going to make some man a nice catch; but she had it in her heart to marry a minister.

Although Carol Anne was probably in the plot from the beginning, she was as embarrassed as K.D. with its execution. Conveniently, K.D. and Carol Anne sat on the same side of the table, across from Mrs. Strommer who kept the evening going with her constant chatter and casual glances. Once in a while, she would pause in her presentations long enough to ask a question, but she couldn't pause long enough for a sufficient answer.

Not really wanting an answer, she asked, "Well, Preacher, are you writing your sermon notes for this week, yet?"

"No," he said casually. "I'm writing a marriage proposal."

In the silence that followed, Carol Anne asked about his girl. And

K.D. enjoyed telling her so much, that the two of them walked out and sat on the porch swing together while he talked about Rebecca and his plans and goals. Then she told him about the pressure of having the best voice in Wheatheart. Because of her talent, she was not really seen as a person, but a machine belonging to the community, always available for weddings, funerals, and church services. She liked K.D. partly because she had not been asked to sing for church services.

K.D. found the rest of the evening pleasant; he enjoyed being with someone his own age and he gained a new perspective on the challenge of his ministry. Wheatheart was not all harvest, hot summer winds, and vicious gossip. He went away feeling like a pastor, at least Carol Anne's pastor.

The next morning, Charlie came early bringing a present—a straw cowboy hat. K.D. tried to reject the gift with politeness, but Charlie wouldn't hear of it. "Ya gotta keep that hot sun off your ears. That's the way you get cancer. Ya can't go running around out there with your head naked."

K.D. knew he was defeated, at least, when he was with Charlie. So he said, rather weakly, and maybe a bit patronizingly, "Thanks, Charlie. You're the best mom I've ever had."

When he put the hat on and looked at himself in the mirror, he had to laugh. He tried not to, but that strange fellow staring back at him with the button-down collar and the silk tie reminded him of a clown he had seen once in a circus in Tulsa. Charlie must have thought it was funny too, because he laughed.

Laughing together, they went out to face their pastoral duties. At the Ericsons, they checked on Abe's comfort and the progress of the plowing. When they stopped at the Benallis to pick up the sandals K.D. had forgotten, they found Vince in the backyard reading *The Confessions of St. Augustine*.

They spent the rest of the day going in and out of stores, farms, and homes, avoiding nothing, not even the John Deere store where Charlie had to go to pick up parts and supplies and to leave a story. At each stop, everyone greeted the new pastor cordially. But he couldn't help but look over his shoulder as he left, wondering what they said about him in his absence.

In the midst of all these other activities K.D. Garrett, scholar as well as pastor, took time to arrange and research his thoughts on the Sonship of Christ from Hebrews 2, the topic of Sunday's sermon.

With both the sermon preparation and his tours with Charlie, K.D. wore himself out. Friday evening, he went to bed just after the sun had set. He lay in the quiet cool darkness and filled his mind with thoughts of pastoring.

The contradictions and anxieties were all still there; this was still Wheatheart, and he was still a stranger in their midst. But somehow he was different now, braver, and freer. Suddenly, he remembered the reason; he had felt that way ever since he had written the letter to Rebecca. Writing that letter pledging his love had not really brought him freedom from the prison he was in, but it had given him a light, a destination to crawl toward.

He wondered why she had not responded; then he remembered that he had not been to the post office all week. How could he have forgotten such an important thing? Just able to catch a glimpse of moonlight coming through the ground level half windows, he checked his watch and saw that he had seven minutes before Earl Bresserman, town cop, barricaded the post office boxes from the night intruders.

Sprinting all the way down, he arrived just as Earl drove up, and managed to get the contents out of the box. Standing under a street light on the north end of Main Street just across the street from what used to be the movie house, he thumbed through the stack of standard stuff until he found the letter. The envelope looked the same as the past ones had, except that he could not find Rebecca's initials on the back flap. In the passion of expectations, he was frightened by that omission before he realized that his fear was unreasonable.

"Just forgot," he said to himself. "Or it's her sense of humor. It doesn't mean anything."

He tore open the letter and devoured each word, each letter, each mark. It read:

Reverend K.D. Garrett, Pastor
First Baptist Church
Wheatheart, Oklahoma
Dear Reverend Garrett:

I am humbled by your pledge of faithful love. Although the pledge itself does not specify any actions on my part, I am nonetheless honored.

But before I can properly entertain the significance of your pledge, I need to ask one further question. Who are you?

Sincerely,
Rebecca Brooks

In the faint light, K.D. laughed because he didn't know what else to do. "The letter is so serious it must be a joke," K.D. thought, but he did not convince himself.

All through Saturday's sermon preparation and Sunday's church service, even during the time he was rejecting the five invitations to Sunday dinner, K.D. still tried to tell himself that the letter was a joke.

He had the words of that letter on his mind when he greeted Mrs. Garland following the service. She was gracious and cheerful, too much so. She thanked him for the service, using the right words and saying the right things. She smiled the appropriate smile, but it was the kind of smile which locked the pastor out of her real world, the world of her feelings hidden somewhere beneath that public face of smiles and cheerfulness.

Back in his room, K.D. continued to tell himself that the letter was a joke, until he sat down with his pen and wrote a response.

21

Notes From a Pilgrim

That Sunday afternoon, Pastor Garrett did not spend time with his books. Rebecca's letter drove him, instead, to read himself. After a time, he took pen and paper, and wrote:

Dear Ms. Brooks:
  My name is K.D. Garrett. I was born in Tulsa, Oklahoma on May 11, 1957. I was re-born in Tulsa, Oklahoma on April 11, 1971.
  I presently function as a scholar at a prestigious monastery in the Southwest. I am temporarily assigned to do penance in a small village in the arid regions of this land.
  The people here are hardened against the Word and noncommunicative with the Spirit. The cries from the tongue of an angel could not penetrate their dullness of hearing.

But he couldn't send that to Rebecca. He pondered, wrote, thought, discarded, and rewrote. Just before the hot wind calmed down and early evening cooled the prairie, he put together his final attempt and sealed it before he had a chance to think again about it.

Dear Rebecca,

I am a struggling pilgrim. I want to serve God more than anything in the world, but to achieve that, I need you.

I am haughty and proud and unforgiving; and I'm prone to want success just for me. In serving God, I sometimes forget what a wise man once taught me. "It's the relationship which counts."

Come go with me. Hold my hand, and together we will discover how to love Him. Then, I will know how to love you.

K.D.

The next morning he mailed the letter.

22

The Ritual of Death

When Pastor K.D. answered a knock on his door the next morning, he came face to face with a stranger. The man was wearing a black, three-piece suit, a white shirt, a string tie with a turquoise clasp, a turquoise belt buckle, and cowboy boots. He was bareheaded. He introduced himself as Curt Waller, from the funeral home.

On K.D.'s invitation, the man came in, bounced up to sit on the bed and delivered his message.

Mr. Hadley had died late yesterday, and the funeral was scheduled for Wednesday afternoon at 2 o'clock. He was a member of the Methodist Church and the Methodist preacher was out of town for two weeks. The family had asked Mr. Waller to arrange for the service. That meant either K.D. or the Pentecostal preacher over in Alva. Would K.D. be interested?

There wasn't much family anymore—a granddaughter, but Mr. Waller didn't know where she lived, and some nieces and nephews; only one of those, Elmer Rich, lived around Wheatheart. There probably wouldn't be more than a handful at the funeral.

The young pastor accepted the request as part of his ministerial and community duty. Then he walked to his office remembering that he had only been to one funeral in his life, and that was in Tulsa. He had no idea what to expect in a town like Wheatheart. But how different could it be? Burying the dead is burying the dead.

Yet, as he went through the day writing and reading, he felt more isolated than ever before in his life. At times he convinced himself that he knew what to do, and he would write rapidly; but then the doubt would come, and he would tear it up and search the Bible, the commentaries, and the concordance again. He didn't seek new ideas from other sources—he had too many of those already. What he needed was confidence, blessing, and he knew whose blessing he needed.

Through skillful telephoning to the state Baptist office, and two different churches in Tulsa, he found Uncle Joe's home phone number.

Uncle Joe wasn't at home, but K.D. was able to speak with Mrs. Warren instead. It seemed that Uncle Joe had gone up to a river near Tahlequah to chaperone a junior high campout. When K.D. heard the report, he mentally added and subtracted and smiled at the thought of this eighty-two-year-old man on the junior high campout. Mrs. Warren was going there herself and she could take a message.

To a woman he hardly knew, but whose husband he loved, he explained his plight as if he were talking to Uncle Joe himself. He couched the report in the immediate, reporting only the present problems and avoiding such topics as small town contradictions, gossip, and people he couldn't reach.

He explained simply the context of the funeral, the awkwardness of a Baptist speaking at a Methodist funeral. How should he conduct himself? What should he say?

Mrs. Warren assured him that she would get the message to Uncle Joe and convince him of its urgency.

After that, he waited. About noon the next day, Ed Rogers from the Culligan Water place called. K.D. had met Ed at the store a couple of times, but he didn't know him that well. For a merchant, he was not very friendly, almost shy, or aloof. In addition to the water store, Ed also ran the telegraph office, a key in his back room. He had a telegram for K.D. The pastor could come get it or take it over the phone.

Not knowing for sure who would have sent him a telegram, but hoping, the pastor chose the telephone option.

Ed Rogers read with no inflection and poorly timed pauses:

"Reverend K.D. Garrett, First Baptist Church, Wheatheart, OK Bury all the Methodists you want to. Preach the Word in season and out. Stop.

Love, Uncle Joe."

Armed with that blessing, K.D. searched the commentaries for new insights and meanings into Christ's death.

Wednesday at eleven o'clock, K.D. went over to the Methodist Church to meet the family, as Mr. Waller had asked. When he got there, he had to check his memory to see if he were on the right day. Instead of a funeral, he found a party in progress. The parking lot was crowded with cars. Although some had out-of-state license plates, most carried just enough patches of red dirt to tell K.D. that they belonged to Wheatheart people.

The whole churchyard was packed with little clusters of people, laughing and talking. Although some of the participants would occasionally move from cluster to cluster, the circles themselves stayed constant. Some of the people were dressed in a cleaner and newer version of what they always wore. Some were dressed in department store formality, and a few wore expensive suits and dresses. Even they mingled from cluster to cluster laughing and talking and sharing memories with only a hint of condescension.

Inside the church, ladies were filling the tables with bowls and pots of food of every kind.

As K.D. stood momentarily bewildered by it all, a voice behind him demanded, "Where's your hat?" K.D. turned and looked into the face of Charlie Brady. Charlie went on without even smiling. "Now, you're just gonna stand around here and down at the graveyard, and let that hot sun cook the tops of your ears and then it'll turn into cancer."

"Why are you here?" K.D. spoke as reverently as he could without whispering.

Seeing no need for reverence, Charlie did not lower his voice or his enthusiasm. "Well, I'm right here, this place, because in a few minutes somebody's gonna ask you to lead in prayer since you're the only Rev here. And then, they're gonna tell you to go through the dinner line first, and I'm gonna be second, because I'm right next to you."

Just as he finished with a grin, Charlie's prophecy came true. As the two of them moved through the line, K.D. asked him again in low tones, "Why the food? Why all this food?"

"Respect for the dead," Charlie told him and everybody else around. "You'll wanna take some of those chicken and dumplings; those are Maud Schwartz's. Be sure to get some of those new peas and potatoes. Mrs. Reinschmidt cooks those better than anybody else. See that currant pie? I bet you've never had any currant pie. It's Mabel Schmidt's, and it's good to eat."

Since he didn't want to ask another question, K.D. only wondered to himself how Charlie knew who had prepared those dishes.

Charlie must have read his mind because he said, "When you've been to as many funerals as I've been to, you just learn these women's specialties. They always bring the same thing. It's part of who they are. You can't go wrong at a funeral meal in Wheatheart."

Since he had not had his first question answered yet, K.D. asked it again as they sat down. "Why are all these people here? Mr. Waller said it would be a small funeral."

"Well, that's the way we are; we do go to the funerals. Some of us come to see kinfolks who used to live around here but moved away. Funerals are good for that. Gives you a chance to catch up on things you're too busy to take care of otherwise."

After that, Charlie introduced K.D. to everybody there, including the nephews and nieces who thanked him for coming.

When the service began, the party ended. K.D. went in early to find a seat which was hidden from view by the display of flowers. He found Carol Anne Bray already seated. She had come early to practice her music with the Methodist organist. From his vantage point looking through the gap between the two sprays, the pastor watched the processional. The townspeople marched in, as if they had just lost a valued friend. Then the family, dozens of them with the nephews and the nieces and all the distant kin, filed in as best they could. Some showed their sorrow by only a grave look on their faces, others wept, and a few were so stricken with grief that they had to have support to make their way to their seats.

Carol Anne Bray sang. One of the nieces read a lengthy biography recounting how Mr. Hadley had come to Wheatheart as an infant with his family in the landrush days, how he had grown to maturity, of his marriage and middle age, how he had suffered through the loss of his wife and his only son, and now, how he had died leaving a host to grieve his passing.

One of the children, a daughter of a niece, read a poem she had written about her great uncle; Carol Anne sang again. Then the young pastor went to the pulpit, and in the language of Uncle Joe, "preached the Word."

For more than forty-five minutes, the pastor of the First Baptist Church reminded the congregation that Christ had died, was buried, and resurrected as the Victor over death.

When the pastor had finished, he marched to the back beside Mr. Waller. There he took his position at the head of the casket as all the mourners marched by to take one final glimpse of Mr. Hadley.

K.D. tried not to watch the individual gestures of sorrow or grief. Most of them looked artificial; and if they were sincere, then they were too personal to be stared at by the public. But still, he noticed the casual glances, the intense looks, even the final kisses, and the tears.

When the last person had filed past, the pastor got into the front seat of a ten-year-old Cadillac hearse, only to discover that the burial was going to be in the Flat Rock Cemetery, twenty-four miles away.

With Mr. Waller and K.D. heading the procession, they traveled down the highway and over the country roads, past fields and farmsteads to Flat Rock Cemetery.

Once inside the air-conditioned hearse, K.D. found Mr. Waller quite pleasant. In language sophisticated enough to communicate with professionals, and country enough to communicate with farmers, Mr. Waller talked of Wheatheart people and the ritual of death. Mostly, K.D. listened, contributing only questions to the conversation; but he had plenty of those, because this day had brought other contradictions.

"I thought you said this would be a small funeral," K.D. said, trying to sound as if he were joking.

"Maybe a few more than I expected, but not many," Mr. Waller answered calmly. "Can't ever tell about these kinds; now with a younger person, say middle-aged, the place would have been packed. That's the way to have a big funeral, die young.

"When we have a lot of people come from out of town, like today, we usually get the local folks. They come to catch up on things, and see people they haven't seen for a long time. Funerals are good for that kind of thing."

"Is that what funerals are, a civic function, a reunion?" K.D. asked, not cynically but from inside, a deep contradiction.

Mr. Waller didn't seem to notice the tone because he had a ready answer, "Oh, no, funerals are for grief. We have to have some formality to express our grief. Either we get rid of the grief or we just carry it around with us.

"Yes," K.D. agreed. "But why did we open the casket? That just seemed to add to the stress."

"But, don't you see?" Mr. Waller went on quickly as if he enjoyed the opportunity. "There has to be some final place where people come face to face with the reality of death. There has been a loss, a separation, and that is what they realize when they come by the open casket."

"But some of those people hardly knew him?" K.D. stated as a question.

"They were grieving not just Mr. Hadley but death itself. When someone else dies, they all feel it, for it reminds them that they aren't going to live forever."

K.D. didn't ask any more questions for a while, but looked out the hearse window at the plows in the fields and the cows in the pastures nursing their half-grown calves. He tried to remember his theology classes at the seminary, but what he had learned there had already turned yellow with age, or maybe had just dimmed with trial. He had studied the theology of death before, but never with as much reality as he had just studied it. And somehow Mr. Waller's lesson made as much sense as any he had ever heard, at least in the present context.

After that, Mr. Waller, bored by the silence, changed the conversation to the topic of the subtle little rituals of the various ethnic and religious groups. "Some of the Mennonite groups down south of here build their own caskets even. We just embalm the bodies for them. Then they conduct their own ceremonies. Beautiful caskets, handmade and sturdy. Better than most I buy. Every denomination is a little different too. Some have more music. Some ministers read straight from a service book. Baptist preachers probably present the longest sermons."

K.D. smiled. "Mine was about average then?"

"No," Mr. Waller said, as he skillfully pulled the long hearse into the narrow gate of the Flat Rock Cemetery. "Your sermon today was the longest I have had in many months."

With this on his mind, K.D. made the interment as brief as possible. He read the appropriate text from 1 Corinthians and prayed for the family, thinking everyone would soon go home to the problems of living. In fact, Mr. Waller whispered in his ear, "We'll go just as soon as people leave. I can't lower the casket in the grave until everyone is gone. You understand, of course."

K.D. nodded yes, although he didn't quite understand; and he waited patiently in the hot sun with nothing to protect his ears for two hours and fourteen minutes until everyone had left and Mr. Waller could lower the casket and ask the gravediggers to cover it with dirt.

K.D. Garrett, Pastor of the First Baptist Church, spent the rest of the evening trying to process all that he had learned. He somehow knew that this had been a significant day for his education, but he did not fully understand what real difference that knowledge and training would make in the way he related to people or even the way he read the Scriptures. He was so occupied with this that he didn't sleep well and was not at all prepared for the lesson he was to learn the next day.

Charlie Brady came early and told Pastor K.D. to put on some old clothes. The two of them had work to do. Fearing the worst, a plowing job or another chance to milk a cow, K.D. pried for more information, but Charlie stood firm. He wouldn't discuss it. He talked about everything else, yesterday's funeral, funerals from thirty years ago, births, rebirths, and steers that got drunk from eating spoiled silage, but he wouldn't talk about today's task.

First they drove out to Wagner's Pond and while K.D. tried to get flat rocks to skip more than five times on the water, Charlie cut small forked branches from a willow tree. They then drove over to the Reinschmidt farm, through the front gate and over to the back side of the pasture. As they bumped and rattled through the pasture, avoiding huge gulleys and boulders, Charlie talked on, but he still wouldn't give K.D. as much as a hint of his strange behavior.

When they arrived at their destination, they stopped and Charlie went to work, only adding to the mystery. He took one of the forked sticks he had cut, held the two ends gently in his fingers leaving the long base sticking up into the air, and he began walking in a straight line. K.D. stood by the pickup, watching and wondering. After a while, with Charlie maybe as much as 200 yards away, he turned around to face K.D. with the end of the stick pointing down to the earth.

"Look, look," Charlie yelled excitedly. "See the stick?"

"Yeah, I see it," K.D. yelled back, not really sure what he was supposed to be seeing.

Charlie must have sensed his lack of interest. "Come here," he commanded. And K.D. sauntered over.

Charlie said, "Now watch this." He turned the stick up, and walked off a few paces. Turning around, he walked back toward K.D. and when he came to the exact spot where he had been before, he turned the stick down again. "See?" he asked even more excitedly. "Didn't you see it?"

"Didn't I see what?" K.D. asked, still dumbfounded.

"Didn't you see the stick turn over?" Charlie asked, elated at what had happened.

"Yeah, I saw you turn the stick over," K.D. said, still not understanding the cause for Charlie's excitement.

"I didn't do it," Charlie yelled. "It turned on its own."

"Why would it do that?" K.D. asked.

"Because there's water down here."

"How do you know?"

"Because the water forced the stick to turn over."

"What?"

"You see," Charlie explained, "I carry this stick. When I walk over a good underground stream, the current down there pulls the end of the stick toward the ground, and then I know that is where the water is."

K.D. laughed and started to walk away. Charlie had told some big stories before, and K.D. was not going to get caught in another of Charlie's hoaxes. He would become the laughingstock of the town, and he couldn't stand that.

Charlie called him back, almost heartbroken. Like a child who has just learned to tie his shoe, Charlie wanted K.D. to appreciate his talent. "I am telling you the truth. This is what I do. People call me the water witcher. When they get ready to drill a well, they call me out to tell them where to drill. You stand there, and I'll show you how this works." Charlie walked away, first in one direction, then in another. Each time as he walked back, the stick turned down at the same spot. After several tries, he drove a yellow stake in the ground and said, "Yep, this is a good spot. Ought to make lots of water right here. I would bet on it." He added the last part still trying to convince the new young pastor.

That night and the rest of the week, K.D. searched the Scriptures and himself like he had never searched before. This time, he wasn't looking for points to win a debate or for sermon topics.

Instead, he was looking for instructions on how to deal with the strange ways, and habits, and deeds of strange people. Before he had known Charlie, had grown to like him and appreciate his wisdom even on spiritual matters, K.D. could have explained away the incident with the forked stick. "A hoax at very best." But since he had seen his friend and colleague perform the deed, those simple explanations weren't enough.

Before he met Mr. Waller and had buried Mr. Hadley, he knew all about death; but since yesterday, he realized that there was more to dying, both for the living and the dead, than he had ever discovered in all his scholarship.

There was more to learn than he knew and maybe more to learn than he could ever know. And that thought drove him into a depth of unscheduled, unplanned prayer. In the tabernacle of his basement room, lying on the bed where old Mr. Strommer had died, he talked with God, and he listened. But all he heard was a silent voice that told him that he didn't understand, and he knew that already.

Although he did not fully regain his confidence in himself before Sunday, he still managed to put together a solid sermon from Hebrews 2 on the common heirship of Christ and man. At times, he thought about changing it in favor of something simpler, discarding the whole Hebrews series, for that matter, but that seemed like the cheap way out. He had made a promise to himself to do the scholarly work those sermons required, and he couldn't back out on that promise.

Since he had prepared thoroughly, the Sunday service itself should have gone without incident, except just before he went into the sanctuary, he found a letter that Mrs. Craig had put in his desk drawer along with the rest of the mail sometime earlier in the week, and he had to go through the entire service, the common heirship, the one-hour greeting at the door, and four dinner rejections, with an unread letter from Rebecca in the pocket next to his heart.

23

Notes From the Prairie

Dear K.D.,

I remember you now. You're the man I love, and you are also the man I want to love me. Thank you for your commitment to love me. I will do everything I can to make it easy for you to keep.

I can hardly wait until the end of the summer when we can sit together in circumstances we both know and make our plans for the future.

Love,
Rebecca

Notes From the Prairie

Dear Rebecca,

I am the metaphor for irony. The circumstances of this week make me humble. I am so inadequate, unschooled even. But your letter reminds me of my great accomplishment. Already, your emotions pour over my emotions to make my life sweeter. You will never know how valuable that is just now.

I still do not understand this place. They are so different from any people I have ever known before. About the time I think I make progress, they show me a new trick, and I start all over again trying to climb out of the pit of confusion.

This week, I have learned to bury the dead and to witch for water; but more importantly, I have learned to know more than what can be taught in the classroom. Let me explain in detail later. Your invitation to plan the future encourages me, and I shall survive my present state of confusion.

Love,
K.D.

24

To Learn the Little Ways

The pastor of the First Baptist Church spent all of the next day catfishing. Delbert Goforth came early with the invitation and K.D. accepted, although he did not know one thing about fishing. He also did not know that Coach Rose was going too. If he had, he would have prepared intellectually. Coach Rose was another of those Wheatheart contradictions. In their chance meetings at the post office through the summer, K.D. had found the coach an unassuming man—quiet, thoughtful, sensitive. But in the Dew Drop breakfast conversations, K.D. had heard of a man with all the trappings of genius—a calculating, manipulative, almost ruthless, one-dimensional, football genius.

K.D. looked forward to getting better acquainted with this contradiction, and he found his first piece of pertinent information when, out of respect for the legend and the man, he offered to ride in the middle of Delbert's pickup seat so the coach could occupy the more prestigious window seat, or "shotgun position" as Delbert called it.

The coach declined with a simple gesture. "No, you may have to open some gates along the way."

But there were no gates, and soon the three men, the coach, the pastor, and the recent high school graduate, had driven the eight miles north to the foot of the hills, and had climbed up to a likely fishing hole in the middle of the river. They baited several hooks with chicken livers and stinkbait, and sat by the edge of the river watching the water and time go by.

The river was almost calm. The summer drought had left the water low. In places where the riverbed was wide, the stream was so shallow that little islands popped through the ripples. In the more narrow places, the water funneled into a current and rushed over the rocks and pebbles. Here and there, some of the water gathered in the holes of the riverbed forming pools.

"That's where the fish are," Delbert had told them. "During the dry times, they hole up in those pools and wait for the rains to come and the river to rise so they can get on with their lives. We should catch a bunch today."

And they did. They spent the day baiting hooks, taking the gray, bullhead catfish off the line, and talking through the waiting times. Although Coach did not talk as much as Charlie would have, he was still filled with information he wanted K.D. to know.

For a long time, he talked about Delbert. With Delbert listening and shaking his head in unbelief at times, Coach told K.D. about how Delbert and his friend, Chuck, through hard work and self-coaching had made themselves two of the finest long-distance runners in the nation.

Then in the big race, Delbert had sacrificed himself with a pace too fast so that Chuck could set the national record. Now Chuck had already gone on to bigger and better things, spending the summer running with some volunteer group in Europe.

Although Coach Rose told the story simply and factually, K.D. sensed that there was more purpose than just the details. This was a story with a moral of integrity, commitment, and unselfishness.

As he thought about it, K.D. began to understand the aura of respect and dignity that the unassuming Delbert carried into the Cafe the morning they went out to plow.

After that, K.D. talked about himself and his seminary education until Coach Rose turned the conversation to a challenging discussion of the realism-nominalism debate in the medieval church, and of Peter Abelard's part in it.

When K.D. asked in pleasant surprise where he learned such things, Coach smiled and said, "I read once in a while."

This wasn't enough for K.D. There was too big of a contradiction between Coach Rose, the man at the catfish hole talking of medieval philosophy, and the man in the minds of the people gathered to eat and gossip at the Dew Drop Inn Cafe.

"How do you make it in this town?" K.D. asked. "Do you just live on the success alone, and hunger for the other things?"

Coach smiled, and talked. He didn't lecture, didn't even talk as an older man to a younger but as one friend to another.

"Success is who you are inside. It has nothing to do with your wins and losses. Regardless of what business you're in, Pastor, success has nothing to do with your wins and losses." He paused and watched the floats bobble in the water before he went on. "I live in Wheatheart because people are the same everywhere. Of course, each culture has its own mores, its own habits, its own ways. Wheatheart is a culture all its own. All little communities may look the same, but they're not. For all their sameness, their cultures are miles apart. For living in Wheatheart, there's a different set of rules than for all the other little towns around. But when you get past those rules, the people are the same. They get born, they live, and they die all alike.

"Think you have a bite, there, Delbert. Yeah, he's a nice one. If you want to meet people in those parts of their lives where everyone is alike, then you have to learn the little ways that make them different. I spent twenty-eight years learning Wheatheart ways; so just to save time now, I stay here."

In addition to everything else he learned that day, Pastor Garrett learned to bait a fishhook, to take a wriggling two-pound bullhead off the line, to cook a catfish over an open fire, and to search for the common thread which weaves all people into one creation.

Utilizing this and other lessons he had learned, Brother K.D. arose before sunup the next day, and drove the white Chevy out to the Ericson's farm.

Since they themselves were just getting up, Abe and Mary Ruth were surprised to see their pastor.

He greeted them by asking, "Can I milk your cow?"

Although they both protested politely, K.D. could tell that they liked the idea. Abe accompanied him to the lot, leaned against the barn, and gave instructions. After a long time of squeezing and pulling, K.D. managed to get a small, weak stream of milk, and he momentarily remembered the first time he rode his bicycle without his father's hand of support. Although he never played tunes on the pail, he still got the milk to flow. Twice he was deterred when the cow, trying to reach some flies just above her hip, smacked him at his shoulders and the back of his neck with her tail.

"Could be worse," Abe grinned. "she could have had scours."

Since K.D. didn't know what the term meant, he decided not to pursue it.

When K.D. had filled the pail to the halfway mark, and all his squeezing and pulling could produce no more, Abe pronounced him finished.

With a sense of pride, K.D. sat and surveyed his accomplishment. The cow, impatient with the delay, started to walk off and put her right rear foot in the bucket. Those feelings of frustration and failure that K.D. had experienced so often over the summer were just about to come back until he heard Abe laughing.

K.D. laughed too. "I don't think I'll ever learn."

"If you ever figure out how to keep a cow from stepping in the bucket, you can tell us all," Abe said. And the two men walked contentedly back to the house where they had a delicious breakfast and pleasant conversation.

On his way back to town, Brother K.D. stopped at three farms just to chat and to check on his people. He spent the rest of the day visiting the stores up and down Main Street, including the John Deere place, listening to the conversation, and joining in when he had something appropriate to say. He even went into the half-walled cubicle which served as Scott Garland's office and talked casually. Part joking and part serious, he invited Scott to church, saying that it would be good for his soul.

Scott's response was a semi-acceptance which K.D. recognized as a total rejection.

"Yeah, I'm gonna get up there some of these days; I've been out of town a lot, but I hear you're a real good preacher."

K.D. started to walk away, but came back with an afterthought, stood over the seated Scott and said, "I sure have come to respect your wife. She is a fine Christian woman. You must love her very much because she loves you very much."

"Good mother too," Scott answered, and spent the rest of K.D.'s time telling him about his son, the quarterback.

Brother K.D. spent the rest of the week in pastoral duties, visiting the people and preparing the sermon, "Lessons Learned While Milking a Cow."

On Sunday morning, Brother K.D. visited all the Sunday School classes for the first time during his ministry there. He just stuck his head into the classrooms, but it was enough for him and the people to acknowledge each other.

Although he enjoyed the song service and especially Carol Anne Bray's special solo, he still was impatient because he was anticipating his time in the pulpit.

Although he had not practiced delivery of this sermon, the words came smoothly and the gestures came naturally. As he recounted the tale of milking Abe and Mary Ruth's cow, the people laughed spontaneously. Most of them laughed not so much at the young pastor, but at the memory of themselves when they had suffered through the same ordeal. Those others, who had never milked a cow, laughed not so much at the young pastor, but at how they thought they would feel if they should ever have the occasion.

By the time Brother K.D. got the cow's foot out of the bucket, the whole congregation was filled with a sense of happiness.

Then he said, "I wonder if our Lord milked goats. Although we have no record of His milking goats, our Lord did all things common to man. He laughed, wept, worked, and went to a grave just like we all do. But then, He arose from that grave and lives now forever just like we can do if we accept Him as Saviour. From that, the young pastor moved the laughing congregation into the realization of Christ's humanity and divinity and what that means to those who worship Him.

Although the church was not as full as it had been in past weeks, it took the congregation longer to leave than ever before. No one stopped to say, "Nice talk, young man." But nearly everyone stopped to tell K.D. a story or to ask a question or to invite him to dinner.

Accepting the first dinner invitation with the Miller's, a farm family out east of town, he was free to listen to the stories and answer the questions.

To contribute even more to the way he was feeling, he was able to find a real solution to one of their problems. On Tuesday, women of the church were going as a group to Cherokee to the district-wide WMU rally. They had planned to use one of the high school girls to baby-sit the children left behind, but she was away at 4-H camp.

"How many children?" K.D. asked, as if he had a plan.

"Eight," the women told him. "Mostly the first-graders and pre-schoolers because the others are old enough to go with their fathers."

"Why, I'll keep them," K.D. offered. "We'll go to the park and play through the day."

With that announcement, everyone at the First Baptist Church went home happy that Sunday afternoon, or at least happier than they were before they came.

* * * * *

When Abe and Mary Ruth drove into the yard after church, their milk cow leaned across the fence and mooed.

"Well, there's the subject of today's sermon," Abe said as they both laughed; and they laughed off and on for years to come when they remembered their young pastor milking the cow and the Lord's humanity and divinity.

* * * * *

During Sunday dinner, Charlie Brady suddenly remembered an incident he hadn't thought about for years. One time—he was just a young man then, must have been still in the 1930s—he was milking a cow which tried to kick him. When she did that, she slipped and fell right on top of him. Both of them, cow and Charlie, lay there scared to death until Hester came over and pulled the cow off. Because there wasn't any damage to either of them, it was good for a laugh.

Charlie enjoyed the memory and the reception to the story so well that he added the story to his repertoire; and everytime he told it, which was often, he also remembered that Christ had laughed, and wept, and worked, and went to the cross for him!

* * * * *

At the Goforth house, the whole family gathered around the dinner table and listened to parents relive the activity of milking cows because neither of the children had ever milked one. But after that, Delbert talked about resurrection.

* * * * *

Mrs. Strommer spent Sunday afternoon going up and down the street visiting house to house, giving advice about the way to raise tomatoes during a drought, gathering information about family matters, and telling about Brother K.D.'s cow-milking experience.

"That young man is going to make a preacher yet," she reported with pride, because she had contributed to the process. "I do think he does better when Carol Anne sings for him, except at Mr. Hadley's funeral. He talked too long and I didn't understand a word of it."

Notes From the Preacher

After the leisurely Sunday dinner with the Millers, K.D. did not have much time left for his letter to Rebecca, but he didn't need much time because the words flowed smoothly and quickly, more out of his heart than out of his mind.

He described in detail the contradiction called Coach Rose, and the joy of catching a catfish. Then, laughing as he wrote, he told her of milking a cow.

From that point he lectured, but he did it with the confidence that came from his knowing that Rebecca would understand.

"I think I have been missing an obvious truth somehow. The simple acts of human experience not only unite us but they also provide a place for us all to begin to understand each other and ourselves.

"This morning I scrapped the Hebrew text which was too deep for them and me, and went with a simple common experience. It is not for me to evaluate. The sermon is now God's to bless. But I do know that I am beginning to understand why I am here.

Despite this, the days drag on because I still miss being with you.

Love,

K.D.

P.S. Pray for me. I practice my baby-sitting skills on Tuesday.

The Pure in Heart

Brother K.D. almost overslept on Tuesday morning because the sun never came up. Sometime during the night, the stars and moon all disappeared under a layer of gray clouds so thick that they looked as if they extended all the way to heaven.

By the time he walked to the church to assume his duties as baby-sitter for the WMU ladies, the clouds had already settled on the horizon in all directions and had drawn the boundaries of the prairie closer than K.D. had ever seen them. It was an unusual sight for him because it was the first day since he had come to Wheatheart that the sun had not shone fiercely, illuminating both the beauty and the harshness of the area. This Tuesday, the dreaded hot winds, always blowing across miles and miles of wheat stubble and baked ground, had turned to northern breezes blowing gently but with a hint of threat.

Just as Brother K.D. and the eight children, three boys and five girls, stood on the top stoop of the church and waved good-bye to the seven carloads of ladies heading to Cherokee for most of the day, the clouds obeyed their impulse and started shedding the water which had weighed them down so heavily.

At first, the rain came almost casually, falling so gently that it hardly made a wet mark on the packed red clay which served as front lawn and parking lot. But soon, the rain came harder and harder until it fell in sheets, turning the whole town into a million little individual rivers running rapidly and at random.

As K.D. stood with the children under the safety of the old wooden awning and watched the rain turn toward torrential, he suddenly had another thought. They weren't going to spend the day happily playing in the park with swings, slides, monkey bars, and space. Instead, like a shepherd of old, he herded his charges to their own basement Sunday School room and relaxed a bit when the children went quickly to the crayons, the books, and the other games they had learned to love during their Sunday School hour each week.

Because they liked the room or because they were good children or because the rain beat on the windows and walls outside, the children clustered in small groups, moving occasionally from group to group, and played or colored through most of the morning. Although K.D. was nervous watching the children play, he managed to look calm enough to invite their questions and pleas for help.

But after Mrs. Craig came and served them all lunch, Kool-Aid and sandwiches, their mood changed as the rain continued to beat down. The children were tired of coloring and playing the usual games, but they were also too tired to rest. As their questions and pleas for help became more frequent and intense, K.D. knew he had to shift the activity to something else. Either by instinct or because of something he had once heard in a seminary class, he gathered them around him, making a very close circle, picked up the first book he could find and began reading. He had hoped for a Bible storybook or even something from the denominational press; but instead, he had picked up *Cinderella*. He liked the selection well enough, but he was afraid of what the mothers might think when they discovered what their children had read in church today. But it was there on top of the stack, so he went on. The story was better than K.D. had remembered it, and soon he was no longer just affecting an entertaining reading. He was into it with all the appropriate motions and emotions. With his voice, he led the children through women's inhumanity to woman, the raw cruelty, the desperation and isolation of the victim. Together they went to the ball with Cinderella and imagined a party grander than any real one could ever be. But somehow they knew this wasn't true joy. It was only an evening. But when the men came with the shoe searching for the perfect foot, the children held their breath, hoping the real princess would get her chance. When she did, they all cheered, and K.D. rested from his reading.

But not for long, because the questions began.

"Why were those old sisters so cruel?"

"Why didn't the mother make them be nicer to Cinderella? My mother would."

"What are ashes?"

"Why was Cinderella so happy even though she had to do all that work?"

"Because she was good." Brother K.D. chose to answer the questions he could, and in doing so maintained some order.

"Are good people always happy?" the child asked.

"Yes," the scholar of God answered confidently, but not knowing for sure why.

"Why did Cinderella get to marry the prince?" the child asked.

"Because she was good," the pastor answered.

"Why didn't the shoe fit the sisters?" the child asked.

"Because they were evil," the young pastor answered.

"That's just like our Bible, isn't it?" the child said.

"I don't think so," the scholar of God answered.

"Oh, yes," the child answered. "In the Bible, good people always get a blessing and bad people always get a punishment."

"Who told you that?" the pastor asked.

"The Bible did," the child answered.

That night, K.D. Garrett read the Scriptures, simply and joyfully. Through the night, he read all the old familiar passages and with one thought in mind, "Blessed are the pure in heart for they shall see God."

Before the night ended sometime past 4 o'clock, he wanted to stay in Wheatheart forever or until he could help all these people see what he had discovered, that good people always do get a blessing.

When he went downtown the next day, he felt his desire to stay was even greater. Without his knowing, the pastor had changed through the night, but the town had changed too.

The sun came up bright like it had every day all summer long; but the rain had washed the red grit and summer dullness from the air so that the sunshine only magnified the blue skies, the green pastures, and the red plowed fields, looking rich and fertile now that they were soaked almost to saturation.

The people poured in from the farms and shopped leisurely from store to store, taking time to remember things they had needed all summer, things like light bulbs and shoelaces and new milk buckets. When they met on the streets, they stopped to talk, taking time to remember things that had happened to them through the summer, things they hadn't had a chance to catalogue in their memories by sharing them with anyone else.

Some talked of bushels and acres; some talked of gardens and half-grown fryers; some talked of football and farm prices; and Charlie Brady talked of the new water well out in the Reinschmidts' pasture.

Brother K.D. spent most of the day moving from conversation to conversation, listening, affirming, joining in where appropriate, adding small talk, laughing at himself and the cow-milking incident, smiling, and somehow managing to keep himself from shouting about the beauty of God's world and His Word.

But maybe he did shout it; because on Sunday, when the people came to church, they wore the same attitude and spirit they had worn to town the day following the rain.

Brother K.D. sensed the spirit and when the pianist played his cue to walk through the passageway into the sanctuary, he was so excited with anticipation that he almost didn't see Coach Rose sitting inconspicuously in the side pew.

Although he knew his gesture smacked of informality, the pastor made his way back to the coach put his arm on his shoulder and whispered, "I'm honored that you're here."

"Had to come," the coach whispered back. "I don't know how to milk a cow either."

When sermon time came, Brother K.D. reminded the congregation that our Saviour said that we must become like children to enter the kingdom.

When he documented his points with his own attempts at babysitting the past week, the people laughed because his stories were as funny as the memories his stories brought back to them.

When the church service was over, the people went home to their Sunday afternoons and daily lives more childlike.

At the door, the pastor accepted the first invitation to dinner and lost count of the others. Coach Rose shook the pastor's hand warmly, bored deep into the pastor's soul with his eyes and said, "You don't have to come to a football practice unless you want to."

27

Notes From the Pastor

My Dear Rebecca,
   This week I have learned that in brevity, as well as in simplicity, is meaning.
   If you were here with me, I could stay here forever.
Consider this and renew your pledge to make our plans together.
   Love,
   K.D.

   P.S. How do you feel about children?

Under an August Moon

Brother K.D. intended to spend the last week of his stay in Wheatheart casually, saying good-bye to all his friends and preparing his final sermon of the summer. But it didn't work out that way.

On Tuesday, as K.D. was making his way along Main Street, Scott Garland came running from the John Deere store, yelling for the preacher's attention. Still not quite comfortable in Scott's presence, K.D. ambled back pleased that this conversation was going to take place in the middle of Main Street with cars and pickups passing by.

But Scott had come to ask a big favor, and he was in a hurry. Tomorrow he was to host the district-wide John Deere territory meeting, an annual affair of more than one hundred John Deere dealers and factory representatives. For the most part, they met for business purposes, to discuss new equipment and marketing techniques, but they also ate and they usually had a speaker, something entertaining. This year, Scott had employed the services of a lawyer over in Alva who could tell jokes and make people laugh. But the man was called back into court on an emergency and couldn't come. Now Scott was without a speaker, and he naturally thought of his friend, K.D., who had had experience speaking before an audience. And besides, Scott had heard about some of his sermons, the cow-milking and baby-sitting ones. Would K.D. consider coming up to the high school gym the next day and talking for twenty to thirty minutes? Tell jokes or stories. Make the people laugh. He didn't want anything serious. Just entertainment.

K.D. responded, "Well, sure . . . " but he didn't get time to say the "but".

Scott grabbed the first two words as a solution to his crisis, and turned to go on about his business. But just to make sure, he turned as he was walking away and said again, "Remember, this isn't the place for any religious stuff. We just want it funny." He turned his back to K.D. before he had finished speaking so that he couldn't see the protest on the pastor's face.

This new assignment interrupted Brother K.D.'s plans and his state of mind. He spent the rest of the day and most of the night preparing not just the jokes but himself for the occasion.

Was this the occasion that the pastor had prayed for, the occasion to talk to Scott Garland, to ask him to make an honest assessment of himself and his actions? Was this a God-given opportunity?

Or was there more to consider than that? Although K.D. had not necessarily agreed to the terms, Scott had assumed that "no religious stuff" was in their contract. Was it now a question of integrity for the pastor to honor that request?

If it was, in fact, the God-ordained moment, and K.D. did not respond to it, he would cheat God and the ministry. On the other hand, if he did not honor Scott's request, he ran the risk of ruining the image of minister in Scott's eyes and perhaps for the other men there, driving the unbelievers among them even further away from a relationship with Christ.

In this dilemma, the young pastor spent the worst night of his summer. Stranded in the isolation of his room, he remembered his Wheatheart career, finding many events almost too painful to recall. He found it hard to believe that he was the person who had, only nine weeks ago, resented the smells, and the dirt, and the talk about bushels and acres. He tried to forget the memory of his own selfishness measured against the people's love, but it wouldn't go away.

Through the night, he struggled with his bed and fought sleep, unable to get comfortable with himself or his thoughts. He even thought of Mr. Strommer dying in that very bed, and he thought of Mrs. Garland.

Through the night and through the next morning, he struggled with that kind of loneliness brought on by the necessity of a decision only he could make.

By the time lunch was served in the high school gym, he sat at the head table trying to keep his stories in mind and searching for a conclusion.

In between his duties as emcee, Scott filled K.D. in on the situations and the surroundings. The tarp on the floor was Scott's idea. He was on the school board and could think of such things. The town simply did not have a place for a dinner of this size. The high school gym seemed like a good idea. All they needed was something to cover the floor

The high school FHA girls were serving the meal. It would be a good fundraiser for them. This was good for the community, a chance to show off the town, the students, and even the Baptist preacher.

After Carol Anne Bray had sung her two songs, a selection from an opera and a rousing medley from *Oklahoma,* Brother K.D. stood and spoke, more relaxed than he could ever remember being in front of an audience. Within seconds, he had those John Deere tractor salesmen and factory reps laughing. Although he had used some of the jokes from the book he had brought from Fort Worth, he basically stayed with his own personal stories of a city boy learning country ways, driving a pickup with a stick shift, plowing corners, milking a cow, and trying to interject his ideas into the John Deere store conversation.

For the most part, the forty minutes were filled with laughter, and time went quickly.

K.D.'s final story about a farmer who had won a million dollars in the lottery and announced his plans for the future by saying, "Well, I guess I'll just go on farming until this is all used up," brought more of an outburst of laughter than K.D. expected. With this response, he didn't know how to get off the stage, so he went on. "I will tell you one thing that's not a joke—Jesus Christ. He is real and His Power can change you. Most of us are not the kind of people we should be—we're selfish, relentless, unforgiving—but Christ can change that." He returned to his seat, and the gym was silent through the few minutes it took a stunned Scott Garland to make his way to the microphone to say, "Let's all take a fifteen-minute break right now. Y'all know where the restrooms are," and Scott walked off to meet his buddies, leaving Pastor Garrett stranded in the middle of the gym floor.

K.D. spent the rest of the day trying to crowd the incident out of his mind with the more pleasant reality of spending time with his friends. But in spite of the good friends he saw—Delbert, Charlie, Coach Rose—he could not free himself from the tyranny of the memory of that moment when he stood in front of all those silent people.

Since he could not forget it, he tried to justify what he had done. "It was God's will," he assured himself. "But if it was God's will, why do I feel so miserable?" Even a fine dinner and a good conversation with Mrs. Strommer could not free K.D. from the agony of remembering.

About ten o'clock, as K.D. sat in his room reading, and trying to escape the dread of having to go to bed, Mrs. Strommer came down to tell him that he had a phone call. He hurried upstairs, expecting bad news. Something had happened to someone in his family, or even worse, to Rebecca. But it was Scott Garland.

"Preacher, I need to talk to you about that thing today," Scott said tersely.

"Sure," the young pastor said, sounding more cheerful and open than he was feeling.

"Not on the phone," Scott said. "What I have to say, I want to look you in the face."

"Okay," the pastor agreed knowing that he had to. "We can meet in my office."

"Your office is the most public place in town," Scott said, rejecting the offer.

"I'll come to your house, then," the pastor said but not really wanting to.

"I don't want you at my house," Scott answered.

"Then where?" K.D. asked, and he would have been impatient if he had not been frightened.

"On the football field," Scott said. "You come to the football field. I'll meet you there."

K.D. decided to walk instead of driving the white Chevy—Scott's pickup. He thought the night air would clear his mind so that he could respond to the challenge he was about to encounter. If he had been wrong, he could offer only a simple apology. But he was not convinced that what he had done was that wrong. And he didn't know how to apologize for an action that was right. For a moment, he even thought of the possibility of violence. But fighting seemed so out of character for Scott Garland that he dismissed that thought. But then he told himself that violence might be easier to respond to than what he was about to hear.

He walked around behind the school, through the open gate of the stadium onto the lush, green grass of the football field he had only seen at a distance. The green natural carpet cooled the night breezes, and they blew gently against his skin.

Although he was not a fan of football, K.D. still felt a sense of awe when he stood on that spot where Wheatheart legends were made, and he began to think about that until he saw Scott Garland walking through the dark from the other side of the field. The two men met in the middle. Although K.D. still was not convinced that he had done anything wrong, he would not knowingly wound any person; so he used his voice to try to soothe the pain which he knew Scott must feel.

Speaking first, K.D. said, "Scott, I'm sorry about what I had to do today."

Although the August moon shone brightly making many things distinguishable, Scott stood with his back to it so that his face was dark and expressionless. The faint sounds of a pickup rattling down Main Street came filtering through the air. Somewhere off to the east, Doc Heimer's old dog, Spencer, barked three times. The air was filled with the aroma of the fertility of new-plowed ground.

Scott spoke, "I have just one question. How do I get saved?"

29

A New Direction

Dear Uncle Joe,

You are the sly one. What a surprise to have Rebecca come to Wheatheart for the last Sunday of my summer interim.

I'm afraid my boyish pride got the best of me as I showed her off to all my friends here. But I think that that might be excusable because I detected some of that same pride as my friends showed me off to Rebecca.

Since we are going to spend our lives together, I'm happy that she was able to see me do what God has called me to do.

I must admit that I was nervous throughout the service, not just because it was my first baptism, but what this baptism will mean to this man's family, to the church, and the whole community.

I doubt that I shall ever know all the reasons why you recommended that I should come here, but I do understand most of them by now. Wheatheart did not undermine my scholarship nor deter me, but it gave me a new direction. Reading Scripture and meeting people can never be a one-dimensional task.

I shall not belittle you with praise, but I will thank you for knowing what I needed and for believing in me.

God's peace be with you.

Your fellow minister,
Brother K.D.

Fiction From Victor Books

George MacDonald

A Quiet Neighborhood
The Seaboard Parish
The Vicar's Daughter
The Shopkeeper's Daughter
The Last Castle
The Prodigal Apprentice

Cliff Schimmels

Winter Hunger
Rivals of Spring
Summer Winds
Rites of Autumn

Robert Wise

The Pastors' Barracks

Donna Fletcher Crow

Brandley's Search
To Be Worthy

Dear Reader:

We would like to know your opinion of **SUMMER WINDS**
Your ideas will help us as we strive to continue offering books that will
satisfy your needs and interests.

Send your responses to:

VICTOR BOOKS
1825 College Avenue
Wheaton, IL 60187

What most influenced your decision to purchase this book?
- ☐ Front cover
- ☐ Title
- ☐ Author
- ☐ Back cover material

- ☐ Price
- ☐ Length
- ☐ Subject
- ☐ Other:_____

What did you like about this book?
- ☐ Hero
- ☐ Heroine
- ☐ Plot
- ☐ Suspense

- ☐ Inspirational theme
- ☐ Romance
- ☐ Adventure
- ☐ Humor
- ☐ Other:_____

How was this book used?
- ☐ For my personal reading
- ☐ Studied it in a group situation
- ☐ Used it to teach a group

- ☐ As a reference tool
- ☐ For a church or
  school library

If you used this book to teach a group, did you also use the accompanying leader's guide? ☐ YES ☐ NO

Please indicate your level of interest in reading other Victor books like this one.
- ☐ Very interested
- ☐ Somewhat interested

- ☐ Not very interested
- ☐ Not at all interested

Would you recommend this book to a friend? ☐ YES ☐ NO

Please indicate your age.
- ☐ Under 18
- ☐ 18-24
- ☐ 25-34
- ☐ 35-44
- ☐ 45-54
- ☐ 55 or over

Would you like to receive more information about Victor books? If so, please fill in your name and address:

NAME:_____

ADDRESS:_____

_____

Do you have additional comments or suggestions regarding Victor books?